Searching for Asia

by
Garey Riester

Escape Artist Productions: 2025 first edition, American Printing Unlimited
Easton, Pa.; 2026 second edition

ISBN: 979-8-9937574-0-7

Images: AI generated art, manipulated, collaged and edited by Garey Reister.

garey-riester.com

Facebook: https://www.facebook.com/garey.riester.9

Instagram: @gareyriester9

Searching for Asia

Searching for Asia

Skimming through a *Newsweek* article Mia finds a photo of a battered school bus and six teenage Asian girls. Looking closer at the photo, she sees that one of the girls looks like her missing daughter, Asia, might look now. Comparing it to family photos, Mia believes the girl in the photo might be her daughter who was kidnapped six years ago in Bangkok.

Returning to Bangkok, Mia will do everything she can including risking her life to find Asia. Does Alan, her soon to be ex-husband, know the truth about Kit, Mia's supposed brother? Does Kit know the truth about Asia and her disappearance? Can Mia convince Sunee, the good Bangkok cop, and Kit that she may have found the location of her missing daughter along with the trafficker that kidnapped her?

Searching for Asia has also won awards as *Virgin Highway* and a variation that takes place in India titled *Breaking the Tiger*.

Introduction

In the last 30 years, I have completed 12 scripts and am still working on four others and have written five art history-related books. Several scripts I have worked on as novels. I have entered my scripts into many film and screenwriting festivals, becoming a multi-level finalist and award winner in 24 festivals, such as Houston, Beverly Hills, Amsterdam, Los Angeles, New York, Boston, etc. I have had two options, but neither made into films. I also had representation through the Gersch Agency in New York.

Through this, I continued to make my art and publish books like my art memoir, *Garey Riester: Strategies of Being*.

It is customary and an unwritten law that a writer does not attach any photos, not even a cover image, to their scripts. I have decided to change that. In my head all these scripts have been made into films. I know the actors I would like for each role. Examples: Walden Goggins and Sam Rockwell in Escape Artist; Jennifer Connelly in this script, Searching for Asia; Kate Winslet and Jon Hamm in Breaking the Tiger, Timothy Ollyfant, Tom Hardy, and Christin Park for Bone Hunters, fun to dream.

When films become hits, scripts are published with photos from the films. I have decided to publish my scripts, add a cover image, and images I have created throughout the text.

I am still hoping that my writing will make it to the big screen. If there is any interest in any of my storylines and/or screenplays, please contact me at g_riester@aol.com or Garey Riester Escape Artist on Facebook.

Enjoy.

FADE IN: SUPER - INT. CHAIN BOOKSTORE WITH CAFE -- CAPE COD -- 2005

MIA DOUGLAS, early-40s, mixed Asian-Caucasian, shoulder-length hair, attractive, wearing a dark cotton jacket, jeans and well-worn boots walks toward a large table of books.

At the end of the table stands ALAN ROTH, Mia's husband, 50-ish, good looking, decent shape, dressed in sweats and a Celtics t-shirt.

Alan looks up and they make eye contact. Mia shrugs her shoulders.

                    ALAN
          The cafe is closed. The $2,500 dollar coffee machine is broken.

Mia picks up one of the books and then with a thud puts it back down.

                    MIA
          How much longer do you think they will be printing books?

                    ALAN
          Kindle, Instagram, Facebook and no one really reads. We skim
          through information... the reason everyone is so fucking stupid.

Mia turns towards Alan.

                    MIA
          Right... and I would like to be able to skim through our divorce
          documents.

MIRROR

Mia's attention turns to a YOUNG TEENAGE GIRL carefully examining her face in a corner vertical mirror.

The girl mugs her petulant lips as her crystal blue eyes catch the reflection of Alan looking at her.

Smiling as if to say, "don't you wish," the young girl turns back to her two GIRLFRIENDS.

Alan exchanges a glance with Mia, whose condescending stare catches him off guard.

Mia walks to the periodical section and quickly picks out two magazines.

                    MIA (CONT'D)
          You're old enough to be her fucking grandfather.

                    ALAN
          My lawyer will have the paper work by the end of--

                              MIA
          I have an idea Alan. Maybe you should write a book instead of
          another wish-I-could-write-a-screenplay script, a skim-through epic,
          Mid-life Crisis for Dummies: Chapter one. I feel so much better
          about my self when I have a twenty-something on her knees in
          front of--

                              ALAN
          Please try to control your self.

The three girlfriends look at each other then walk away.

                              MIA
          You know one of the real emotional differences between men and
          women?

                              ALAN
          No, but I guess I am about to hear.

                              MIA
          Men fall in love with their eyes, with what they see and touch.
          Women fall in love with their ears, with what they hear and with
          the words they chose to remember...

Alan picks up another book opens it and closes it, wishing he was not there. He
picks up the original book he had and walks away.

Mia, still carrying the two magazines, walks behind Alan as they head toward
the checkout.

                              MIA (CONT'D)
          What was the real number of your indiscretions?

                              ALAN
          You are the one who chose to live your life on the road.

                              MIA
          Please... The less we have to say to each other the better.

INT. CHECKOUT - CONTINUOUS

Mia puts the two magazines on top of Alan's book. Top cover on *Newsweek*.
Headline "Virgin Highway."

                              MIA
          So, when are you finally going to marry the trophy bitch? What was
          it again that she did for a living?

          (louder)

Oh yes, I almost forgot. She was a trainer, our trainer.

The CASHIER, a twenty-something female with blue hair and a nose-ring looks awkwardly at Alan.

                              MIA (CONT'D)
          This poor girl thinks she is watching an episode of *Jerry Springer*.

Mia snatches the magazines before the cashier can bag them. Mia and Alan head toward the exit.

The young cashier flips them the finger.

Alan looks at Mia somewhat affectionately as they head toward the parking lot.

EXT. PARKING LOT - CONTINUOUS

The sky is gray as steady rain falls. Alan opens an umbrella and offers it to Mia. Mia shakes her head no.

Mia steps out into the rain.

                              ALAN
          Are you still taking your medication?

                              MIA
          Can't you tell?

Mia smiles as Alan turns and walks away.

Mia looks up into the downpour as rain caress her hair and face.

INT. KITCHEN - TWENTY MINUTES LATER

Mia slams the kitchen door shut, picks up mail from the floor places it on the counter, along with the two magazines.

Mia tosses her jacket to a near by chair and goes to the other counter and pours herself a scotch.

INT. KITCHEN - A FEW MINUTES LATER

                              MIA
          Shit.

Mia picks up the *Newsweek*. She begins to casually look through the magazine. Mia downs her scotch.

Mia stops at the "Virgin Highway" article, reads a bit of it, skims through, then stops and goes back to a photograph on a previous page.

She focuses on a black-and-white photo of six ASIAN TEENAGE GIRLS standing in front of a battered school bus. Alongside is a twenty-something MALE having what looks like a conversation with a young FEMALE POLICE OFFICER.

Mia looks closer, suddenly she rips the page from the magazine and walks quickly toward another room.

INT. BEDROOM - CONTINUOUS

Mia goes to the window and pulls the curtain open as daylight fills the room. To the left of the window is a wall with a number of framed photos.

Mia lights a cigarette and goes to the wall. Mia takes a hit and slowly eyes the photos.

One photo of what looks like a devastated African village. Mia is walking with two young black soldiers and she is holding a over-sized professional camera.

Another photo of her in battle fatigues, taking photos of soldiers firing out of a bunker.

Another photo of her in a post-battlefield landscape, speaking with two distressed Arab women.

She puts the cigarette back between her lips and focuses on a photo of her, Alan and a girl about 12-13 years old. Looks like a happy moment in time.

She picks up the black-and-white magazine photo, folds it so it only shows one of the girls and compares it to the family photo.

Putting out the cigarette, she removes the photo from the wall and with both photos goes back to the window.

With the daylight from the window, she compares the photos again.

The *Newsweek* photo is of an older girl, but the two girls, the girl from her family photo, do look alike.

Mia back steps and falls onto the bed.

Mia begins to gently cry as she holds the magazine photo to her chest.

                              MIA (CONT'D)
          Fuck!

INT. BANGKOK - DON MUEANG INTERNATIONAL AIRPORT - 6 MONTHS EARLIER. - OVERVIEW

INT. WAITING AREA - CONTINUOUS

JADE, Asian, in her mid 20s, turns and hands the deck to a slightly overweight FEMALE FLIGHT ATTENDANT.

A female hand with perfect red finger nails slowly flips through a flush of passports.

Opening the passports the attendant walks along the first row of TEENAGE
FEMALES. Two of the girls smile and nod their heads.

Seated a few seats away is NOON, in his late teens, jet black hair, deep red
lipstick, gives the attendant a fuck you smile as she ties her hair in a
ponytail.

                         FLIGHT ATTENDANT
          This is a football team?

                         JADE
          One of the best soccer teams in Thailand.

                         NOON
          Number one!

                         FLIGHT ATTENDANT
          You're not going with them?

                         JADE
          No. Our coach left a few days ago. The paperwork got somewhat
          complicated.

The flight attendant flips through the rest of the passports as if she is
suddenly in a hurry, not really matching them with the seated girls.

The girls begin boarding the plane. Two of the girls turn to wave. Jade is
already gone.

INT. AIRCRAFT - MINUTES LATER

The female FLIGHT ATTENDANT tries to get everyone seated as additional
passengers board.

GIRL seated next to Noon.

                         GIRL
          Where's Paris?

The attendant, surprised, smiles and continues down the aisle.

                         FLIGHT ATTENDANT
          Don't I wish.

Noon looks at her like she can't believe the question.

                         NOON
          Paris is in a country called Europe.

ANGELINA, in her late-teens, wearing a Madonna T-shirt, makes eye contact with Noon.

                              NOON (CONT'D)
          What's your name?

                              ANGELINA
          Angelina, and Paris is a city in a country called France.

Noon gives Angelina a smart-ass look.

Angelina turns to the window to watch the flurry of activity outside.

EXT. GATE AREA - SAME

A police vehicle with lights flashing rests 20 yards from the aircraft. A school bus pulls along side the police vehicle.

An attractive female police officer, SUNEE, along with two MALE Officers, head toward the ramp as it's being pulled away from the plane.

INT. AIRCRAFT - CONTINUOUS

Sunee flashes her badge and then works her way down the aisle of the aircraft.

                              SUNEE
                              (THAI)
          The girls who are on the football team will follow the two officers
          off this aircraft!

The girls look confused.

                              SUNEE (CONT'D)
          Now, lets go!

The girls begin to follow the officers off the aircraft.

                              NOON
          Paris?

                              SUNEE
          I guess you'll have to see Paris another time.

EXT. DEPARTURE AREA - CONTINUOUS

The girls are herded toward the open doors of the weathered school bus.

A 30-something, Cambodian male, MOOKIE, with a pock-marked face and earring, stands at the open door as the girls are ushered onto the bus.

Sunee approaches speaking loudly to Mookie. The sound of another aircraft taking off drowns out her voice.

A camera flash by another OFFICER, the photo seen in the *Newsweek* is taken.

Mookie smiles and nods his head as Sunee hands him a piece of paper.

Sunee turns and heads back toward the police vehicle. The police vehicle pulls away.

INT. BUS - MOMENTS LATER

Angelina looks out the bus window at the aircraft they just left.

AIRPLANE

The side of the aircraft reads: Uzbekistan Airways.

EXT. ROADWAY - TROPICAL LANDSCAPE - FOLLOWING MORNING

The weathered school bus travels along a rural tropical highway. Deserted beach and ocean on the left side of the road.

INT. BUS - SAME

Empty water bottles, food wraps, and spoiled fruit litter the rusted floor area of the bus.

Cell phone RINGS. Mookie answers it.

                    MOOKIE (THAI)
          No, it's fucking Brad Pitt.

Behind him a few of the girls sleep while others stare out windows. One girl nods her head to music coming from headphones.

Mookie looks at the girls and smiles.

                    MOOKIE (CONT'D)
          I got... (He counts with his head) I got fifteen girls. We tell Lee
          they got hijacked.

BUS SEAT

Angelina sits looking out the window as the blur of the rural roadside passes.

                    MOOKIE (O.C.)
          Fuck Lee. I have a bus load of ripe fruit. You know the price. I'll
          be there in the morning.

Noon plays with her cell phone.

Angelina glares at Mookie as he continues his conversation.

                    MOOKIE (CONT'D)
Fuck you! No, no! You can make that back in a week with just one of them.

INT. BUS SEATS - CONTINUOUS

Angelina looks at Noon.

                         ANGELINA
          You know where this asshole is taking us?

                         NOON
          Not sure. With the police involved probably a shelter.

Angelina turns and stares hauntingly out the window as the bus continues along
the shoreline.

                         ANGELINA
          How you get here?

Noon smiles and shakes her head.

                         NOON
          Village had too many girls. You?

No response.

Angelina puts on head phones and stares out the window acting as if she didn't
hear the question.

EXT. SHIT ROAD - MORNING

The bus makes a sharp turn and enters what's left of a soccer field in the
middle of nowhere. A light rain is falling.

The bus door opens.

                         MOOKIE
          Let's go ladies.

The girls begin to exit behind Mookie. Mookie holds an open plastic bag. The
girls who have cell phones drop them in the bag.

EXT. SOCCER FIELD - CONTINUOUS

To their left rests a small roadside village and in the foggy distance what
looks like army vehicles.

JOY, in her late twenties, shoulder length hair with a white streak of bangs, a
Guns & Roses T shirt, tight shorts, with a very athletic body, several tattoos
on her arms and legs, and a scar across the right side of her face heads toward
Mookie and the girls.

                         JOY (THAI)
          When was the last time these girls had anything to eat?

                              MOOKIE
              I don't run no fucking resort. (laughing)

They walk. They talk.

Joy pulls up a few of the girls shirts. Then, she looks at a few of their arms
for needle marks. Joy holds out her hand to Mookie. He smiles and gives her a
plastic bag filled with their passports and cell phones.

Noon pauses for a moment and stares at the muddy field and river to their
right. Angelina follows Noon's eyes.

TWO MEN, early 30s, partially dressed as soldiers, approach. Noon pokes Angelina.

                              NOON
              Paris trip a lie, like always and this is no shelter... and we don't
              want to be here.

A 30-something, EASTERN EUROPEAN/THAI, JIMME SON, a Johnny Depp wanna-be,
wearing blue-tinted shades comes into view from behind the girls.

He stops in stride and smiles at one of the younger girls, pausing he runs his
hand through her dark hair. She pulls away.

                              JIMME
              Any of you pretty things speak the good Lord's English?

Noon looks at Angelina. She shakes her head no. Both girls remain quiet.

The unrestrained sound of Mookie and Mic arguing in the background.

                      JIMME (THAI) (CONT'D)
              Good afternoon, lovely ladies. My name is Jimme Son. There has
              been a change of plans in regards to your trip. Some good friends
              of mine decided you are much more valuable here, and safer, here.
              The flight to Paris was a lie.

Jimme walks slowly in front of the two lines of girls.

                          JIMME (CONT'D)
              It was a flight to a not so lovely place called Uzbekistan. A very
              nasty man had decided to buy a plane load of young girls that he
              needed to make him and his friends back home happy.

Jimme stops in front of Angelina.

                          JIMME (CONT'D)
              So now you will be safe with me and my men... until we find a
              safer, more productive way to put you back out there in the real
              world.

Jimme gently holds Angelina's head with his hand.

                         JIMME (CONT'D)
          What is your name?

Angelina stares at him and says nothing.

Jimme smiles at Angelina then snaps his fingers and one of the other soldiers
pulls a girl out of line and drags her away.

                         ANGELINA
          My, My name is Angelina.

Jimme steps closer and rubs his had up under her t-shirt and over her breast.

                         JIMME
          So you do speak English. I'm going to give you new name. There is
          always one girl that...

The yelling between Joy and Mookie gets louder.

Two other MEN take two girls, one over his shoulder, the other reluctantly
walking alongside the other man, back toward the village and toward a large,
one-story pink building.

Jimme is annoyed at the sound of Mookie's voice.

                         JIMME (CONT'D)
          The tattooed woman over there, (he points) is named Joy, when we
          are done here Joy will take you to your new housing, feed you, give
          you some clean clothes. Later, I will come by to get a good look
          at each one of you.

Jimme turns and heads toward Joy and Mookie as they continue to bicker over
payment.

Jimme separates the two of them.

                         MOOKIE
          Bullshit! Mr. Lee pays a minimum of 500 per girl.

                         JOY
          No, this is what I pay you. Nothing more. Go away, you look and
          smell like pig shit.

                         JIMME
          You're now selling wholesale. The economy sucks. Not so many farang.

                         MOOKIE
          Bullshit! Bangkok filled with farang looking for girls. I take
          girls back. No sale!

Mookie starts to walk toward the line of girls.

Jimme grabs him turns him around and punches him in the head repeatedly. Mookie falls to the ground. Jimme throws the money at him.

                              JIMME
          Get your sorry ass out of my village. The next time you see Lee...

Jimme kicks Mookie a few times.

                         JIMME (CONT'D)
          The bus got hijacked. Show him your bruises!

BACK TO LINE OF GIRLS - SAME

Noon nudges Angelina.

                         NOON (SOFTLY)
          The river.

Angelina gives Noon a blank stare.

Noon suddenly breaks toward the river. Angelina hesitates then follows.

RIVER BANK - CONTINUOUS

                              JIMME
          Son of a bitch!

Angelina and Noon run then stumble down a stone and mud embankment. Noon hits the water first.

                              NOON
          Come on!

Jimme and Mookie give chase.

Angelina pauses at the edge of the river.

                         ANGELINA (ENGLISH)
          (softly to herself) I can't swim.

Jimme watches Noon fight the current and pushes Mookie into the water.

Mookie swims awkwardly. Noon is no where to be seen. Joy scans the surface of the river.

Joy looks to her left. Foot prints.

Angelina, holding her breath, lies in a patch of bamboo a few feet below the surface of the water.

Angelina breaks the surface of the water gasping for air. Joy stands over Angelina. Jimme stands a few feet away.

                              JIMME
          Sweetheart, you been watching too many Rambo movies.

Joy pulls Angelina out of the mud and begins to SLAP her.

                         JIMME (CONT'D)
              Stop!

Angelina spits at Joy.

Jimme pulls Angelina's wet mud streaked hair away from her face.

Angelina forcefully shakes her head as water splatters on the Joy's face.

                    JIMME (ENGLISH) (CONT'D)
          An-ge-lina... They name you after very beautiful woman. You have
          new name now, Angel. (He looks at Joy) (THAI) Take my little angel,
          clean her up, feed her, then bring her to my place. My next film
          now has a new star.

                            JOY (THAI)
          You pull that shit again, I make your tight little ass wish it
          already died and went to heaven.

Joy pushes Angel up the embankment. Mookie staggers out of the water behind Jimme.

                            MOOKIE,
              She gone, maybe she drowned.

Jimme turns around and hits Mookie again in the head. A beaten Mookie lies in the mud.

Joy and Angel, followed by Jimme, head back toward the village. Mookie looks at the blood on his hand.

                        MOOKIE (SOFTLY)
              Mr. Lee not going to be happy you stole his girls.

EXT. HOTEL ROOM - BANGKOK - NIGHT - TWO WEEKS AFTER *NEWSWEEK* PHOTO

Mia runs her hand through her dark shoulder-length hair as she exits the bathroom with a towel loosely wrapped around her torso.

The room is bare. A CREAKING ceiling fan provides a limp breath to the room. A jug of water and a bottle of Scotch with maybe two shots of liquor left, rest on a small table next to a disheveled bed.

Nightstand. Mia pops open a bottle of pills.

SMALL TERRACE

Downing the pills with a half filled glass of scotch, Mia looks out at one of the seedy brightly lit back streets of Patpong in Bangkok.

Mia drops the towel as she walks back into the room. On her back at her right shoulder is the perfect tattoo of a walking tiger.

Behind her a wall covered with push-pinned photos of young Asian women.

DESK

Mia sits down with her laptop. Next to the laptop is a photo of a young girl, a cropped enlargement of the photo from the magazine. To the left of the photo are a number of copies of the same photo.

She clicks in as a new typed document fills the screen. Page 3. She begins to type.

VISUAL OF PATPONG

A neon-lit maze of crowded pedestrian traffic, scooters, carts, and mostly male tourists.

                         MIA (V.O.)
          Much of Bangkok is like an intoxicating slut that you keep trying
          to convince yourself you have had enough of, yet keep coming back
          to. This slut of a city shimmers with an aroma laced with burning
          petrol, liquor, and cheap perfume.

(MORE)

                         MIA (V.O.) (CONT'D)
          This intoxicating aroma floats like a golden brown halo above
          block after block of noise and neon. A misogynist maze of crime,
          flesh, drugs and money in the City of Angels. A quarter of a
          million sex workers. 80% under the age of 18.

          In 2014, only 180 arrests for trafficking. Convictions? Cold cases
          here are all but frozen.

VISUAL CONTINUES

Club after club filled with scantily clad females on door steps. Standing in lines on the street. Looking like clones of each other. Many of them look no older than 14 or 15

                         MIA (V.O)
          I have returned to Bangkok determined to find what was stolen
          from me.

KNOCK on her door.

Mia puts on a silk robe, closes her laptop, and opens the door.

Alan and Mia face off.

                    MIA (CONT'D)
          I thought I made it clear I never wanted to see your fucking face again!

Mia slaps him across the face.

Alan gently pushes her away and closes the door.

                    MIA (CONT'D)
          How did you know where I am?

                    ALAN
          An e-mail from Keith Ford.

                    MIA
          That cock-sucker.

                    ALAN
          Someone from *Rolling Stone* tipped him off. Said you're doing a story
          on spec.

                    MIA
          A little something to try and get back on the fucking map.

                    ALAN
          You just pack-up and vanish?

Mia freezes as their eyes meet. Mia puts on sunglasses and picks up an empty
bottle of scotch.

                    MIA
          What are either of you two assholes doing in Bangkok?

                    ALAN
          He's working for some lefty foundation. George Rose.

                    MIA
          The last time he tried to help anyone, they almost all got killed!

                    ALAN
          He did get you out alive.

                    MIA
          No, all bullshit. I got myself out. He knew I was going to bury his fat ass.

Mia sits some what reluctantly at the end of the bed.

Alan sits in a chair across from her. He stares at the wall of stapled photos.

                         MIA (CONT'D)
          Every day I wake up asking myself why we gave up.

                         ALAN
          It's been over six years.

                         MIA
          Don't start giving me your bullshit about the odds.

                         ALAN
          We spent close to a year and not one clue. Nothing else we could
          have done.

Alan's attention goes back to the wall of photos. Each photo a wondering, moving
portrait, each having its own personal emotional, confrontational resonance.

                         ALAN (CONT'D)
          It's hard for you to take a bad photo.

                         MIA
          I guess that's why they printed books of my work.

Mia walks toward the mirror. She removes the sunglasses.

                         MIA (CONT'D)
          This mirror reflects as if it's aghast at the sight of me. A
          reflection that persists in trying to convince me that what I'm so
          desperately trying to find, and maybe risk my life for, is gone.

Mia drops a color, 8x10 photo in Alan's lap.

                         MIA (CONT'D)
          Part of a *Newsweek* article I found a few weeks ago. The Barnes and
          Noble episode. I like that... We do now live in episodes.

Alan looks at the photo.

                         MIA (CONT'D)
          The girl on the left.

                         ALAN
          Could have been taken five, six years ago or six months ago.

                         MIA
          Look at the fucking photo... the billboard behind them.

A billboard for *Lost in Translation*.

                              MIA (CONT'D)
          Look at her. She's not Thai.

                              ALAN
          This fucking city was like the United Nations after the war.

Alan walks along the wall of photos.

                              ALAN (CONT'D)
          You came back to Bangkok because of a girl in a photo?

                              MIA
          I came back to Bangkok to find our daughter and to bring her home.

She clicks off the lamp at her night stand.

She pauses, then reaches for the bottle of scotch on the side table. She downs
the trickle that remains. Mia glances across the room toward the windows.

Alan now sits in a wicker chair on the open terrace.

                              ALAN
          This feels like Saigon, when it seemed you could cut the air with
          a fucking knife.

Mia picks up a comb, and pulls it through her thick hair.

                              MIA
          Saigon sometimes feels like it was yesterday and sometimes like it
          was...

Alan turns around and stares at her.

                              ALAN
          It was another life. A life you were lucky to have escaped.

                              MIA
          Do you want me to thank you again?

Alan gets up from the chair.

                              ALAN
          Your therapist?

                              MIA
          None of your damn business.

Mia lets her silk robe fall to the floor. She wears panties but no bra.

                              MIA (CONT'D)
          Just a physical erotic flashback... and don't even think about it.

                              ALAN
          We will leave it as my cue to tell you what a great ass you have
          for a woman in her mid-forties.

                              MIA
          Remember, lover boy, I'm Asian. Aging well is part of the DNA.
          One of the reasons white guys like you chase after Asian pussy.
          (exaggerated younger voice) And I love you so much... You must be
          a good man. Me no love your money just you... A la Saigon and the
          lovely Bang-cock. Perfect name for the City of Angels and sex.

Mia smiles as she seductively picks up her bra and puts it on.

                              ALAN
          Have you seen your long-lost brother yet?

                              MIA
          Why do you still hate him so much?

                              ALAN
          We came to Bangkok six years ago to see your brother.

Mia buttons the last button on her blouse and directs her attention to his
reflection in the mirror.

                              MIA
          We had not seen each other for close to 12 years. He was the only
          family I had left.

Mia turns and empties her make-up bag onto the bed, finds her pills, and pops a
few. Swallows with difficulty with no water.

Alan steps in from the terrace.

Alan picks up the framed portrait from her desk. He walks to the wall and
compares that photo to the pictures stapled to the wall.

                              ALAN
          This is a bit obsessive.

She takes the photo from his hand.

                              MIA
          You're the one that convinced us to leave.

She goes to a table and picks up another group of photos and a large stapler.
Manic-like, she staples the photos to the wall next to her bed.

                              ALAN
          Again, have you seen him yet?

                              MIA
          I told him the next time I wanted to hear from him was when he
          found my daughter... our daughter.

She stands a few feet away and visually consumes the wall of photos.

                              MIA (CONT'D)
          You convinced me that I had closure. I don't.

Mia stares at Alan with a 'fuck you' smile as he walks toward the room door.

                              ALAN
          You do know how many girls are out there?

                              MIA
          Until someone stops me, I'll keep taking their fucking pictures.
          Most of the sex clubs have a type of sexy uniform their girls
          wear.

          Easier to go back and try and find a girl if a photo looks like a
          possibility.

                              ALAN
          Do you think these club owners are just going to allow you to play
          journalist and continue asking questions and taking photos?

                              MIA

          Asking questions and taking photos was what I once did for a
          living.

Alan closes the door and exits down the hotel hallway.

INT. HOTEL - UPSCALE PARTY - FOLLOWING NIGHT

High-end ballroom richly littered to the max.

Mia stands alone. Her only companion, a half empty glass of scotch.

Mia surveys the ballroom inhabitants, a racial and ethnic mix of Bangkok elite,
and foreigners. Her eyes pause and refocus.

KEITH FORD, late 50s, a large man, looking like he is about to take root, leans
against the bar.

Mia approaches the bar and sits two bar stools away from him.

                         KEITH
          So what brings you back to Sin City?

                         MIA
          Maybe to do a story about assholes like you.

                         KEITH
          Sweetheart, I'm here working for one of your liberal heroes.

                         MIA
          I thought Soros would do better due-diligence.

                         KEITH
          We're both working on the same side for the same team.

Keith smiles as he toasts Mia. Keith has obviously had one too many.

                         KEITH (CONT'D)
          I take it, that it is your desire to write a piece of journalism
          with photos that exposes the night mare and 'the horror of all of
          this'...

Keith doing a bad Brando

                         KEITH (CONT'D)
          Oh the horror... the horror.

Keith downs the rest of his drink

                         KEITH (CONT'D)
          A memorial to your missing daughter that may get you published
          again.

                         MIA
          Fuck you!

Keith looks back to the bartender.

                         KEITH
          We're running on empty.

Two drinks are placed on the counter.

                         MIA
          Who's event?

Keith nods and motions with his head toward an attractive couple.

Mia seems somewhat startled.

                              KEITH
          Kit Lee. He just gave a bunch of money to help build a new school
          for runaways, abandoned future would-be skin-joint material.

KIT LEE, in his early 40s, wearing a black suit and tie, with the lovely JADE,
later twenties, long black hair at his side, head toward the bar.

                              MIA
          Kit Lee?

Keith takes another drink from a passing tray.

                              KEITH
          Once was one of Bangkok's finest.

Keith sips from his drink and nods towards Kit.

                              KEITH (CONT'D)
          The exotica standing next to him is the lovely Jade. One of the
          girls he supposedly rescued. He owns the Pink Cherry a few blocks
          away in Patpong.

                              MIA
          I guess in your English dictionary, exotica refers to a lovely
          twenty-something with perfect tits and ass.

                              KEITH
          What gambling is to Vegas, those tits, ass and rose-shaped lips
          between her legs are to Bangkok.

Mia continues to stare at the couple. She downs another drink.

                              KEITH (CONT'D)
          Only place you can get a 15-year-old virgin to sit on your face for
          sixty Euros. Spotless, free of HIV.

                              MIA
          Knowing you, that must come from first-hand experience, and way,
          way too much information.

Keith looks at Mia's figure. Mia motions for another drink.

Kit and Jade are half way to the bar. Mia can't keep her eyes off of them.

                         KEITH (LEANS OVER & WHISPERS)
          He works both sides of the highway. We sometimes work together.

                              MIA
          The highway?

                             KEITH
          Trafficking. The proverbial skin trade.

Mia and Kit lock eyes then Kit turns towards Keith.

                              KIT
          What are you drowning yourself in tonight?

Kit steps towards Keith.

                             KEITH
          Kit Lee and the lovely Jade. I'd like to introduce Mia Douglas, one
          time journalist for...

Mia reluctantly smiles. Kit pauses, smiles and they shake hands.

                              MIA
          Actually, I now work freelance.

The bartender puts two drinks on the bar. Mia takes one of them.

Jade motions in the direction of a young, lovely RED HAIRED WOMAN, Caucasian.

                             JADE
          Excuse me, I have to take care of some business.

Jade exits.

Mia stands next to Kit.

                              MIA
          What a beautiful young woman!

                              KIT
          A business associate.

Mia seems hesitant then whispers to Kit.

                              MIA
          Our alcoholic friend told me you're no longer a cop.

                              KIT

          Let me show you one of the best views of our lovely city.

Kit and Mia walk toward a balcony that overlooks much of Bangkok.

Mia hesitantly turns around and stares at Kit as if six years ago was yesterday.

DISTANT BAR

Keith raises his glass to them and toasts.

BALCONY - CONTINUOUS

                              KIT
          It's been a very long time.

                              MIA
          Your change of profession, is it because you took too many bribes
          or because you didn't take enough?

Kit stares out at the bright lights of Bangkok.

                              KIT
          How is Alan?

                              MIA
          We're in the process of getting a divorce.

Kit turns and steps back from Mia.

                              MIA (CONT'D)
          Keith Ford.

                              KIT
          You two have a history.

                              MIA
          If I had my way he would be fucking history. Does he know about us?

Kit shakes his head no.

                              KIT
          Why did you come back?

                              MIA
          I need to start writing again... I need to find our daughter.

They stand looking through each other for a moment.

                              MIA (CONT'D)
          My daughter. I found a photo. A girl in the photo could be...

                              KIT
          She was 12-years-old... She would now be 18. Very different.

Mia stares at Kit like she is lost.

                              KIT (CONT'D)
          You will have to excuse me. I have to get back to my guests.

                                   MIA
          I'm at the Oberoi.

Kit gently kisses her on the forehead then turns and walks away.

EXT. PATPONG - SILON RD - LATER

Mia, wearing a linen jacket and jeans, strolls through the crowded main streets
of Patpong, the main night-club, red- light strips of Bangkok.

THE STRIP

The sidewalks are lined with gaudy, brightly lit facades.

Young boys proposition the male street traffic with exotic tales of the girls
inside. Some flash photos.

A choreographed troop of teenage girls, vampire-like, dart in and out of
brightly-lit doorways.

Mia stops a pimp and one of his girls. She shows them a photograph. The pimp
and the girl both shake their heads no.

Another PIMP leans over, attempting to snatch the photograph from Mia's grasp.

                                  PIMP
          Come see beautiful girls.

Mia focuses on a facade across the street.

EXT. FACADE - PINK CHERRY - CONTINUOUS

Mia crosses the street toward the Pink Cherry.

Neon lights encircle the doorway and canopy, flashing to the beat of ELECTRO -
POP MUSIC. The backside of a girl not more than five feet tall, very thin and
in a g-string bikini, lights a cigarette.

Mia approaches her.

                            MIA (ENGLISH)

          Can I talk to you? Do you speak English?

Noon turns around.

Mia carefully removes a photo and holds it out for Noon to see, as an older pimp passes with three teenage girls. He gives Noon a cold stare.

Noon looks at him, then back at the street. She hands the money back to Mia and pushes the photo away.

Mia studies the other girls. One of the girls, NOON, maybe 18, blue and pink streaked hair, turns around. She then takes the photo from Mia.

                              NOON
          This not the place to ask questions. One day you here, next day
          vanish like you never exist.

Her pimp turns around and pulls her away.

                              NOON (CONT'D)
          Girls like me?

Noon grabs the photo from Noon and gives the pimp the finger.

                              MIA
          I'm looking for someone.

Noon looks at the photo then hands it back to Mia.

                              NOON
          Did you listen to what that little bitch just said?

Mia looks around and removes a number of bills from her pocket.

                              MIA
          I'm working on a story about girls like you.

Noon pouts coyly and takes the money. Mia raises the photo toward Noon's face.

Noon reluctantly looks at the photograph, the photo of the group of girls seen earlier. Noon says nothing.

                              MIA (CONT'D)
          My name is Mia.

                              NOON
          Noon.

A YOUNG POLICE OFFICER leans over trying to look at the photograph.

                              OFFICER (THAI)
          Are we having a problem?

Mia puts the photo under her jacket as Noon steps between the cop and Mia.

                              NOON (THAI)
     She got husband back at hotel. She like to watch her husband fuck
     young girls.

Mia gives both of them a dirty look.

The officer looks at Mia, smiles, nods, then slowly walks away.

Noon grabs Mia's arm. They walk a few yards then turn into a side street.

                              NOON (CONT'D)
     I get paid for sex. This is not the place to be asking any other
     questions then what I'm willing to do and how much it costs.

Noon snaps her fingers. Mia again shows her the photograph.

                              NOON (CONT'D)
     Those girls imports. Chinese, maybe Cambodia, some look like Oreo.

Noon looks at the photo closer.

                              NOON (CONT'D)
     Two of them maybe.

                                   MIA
     Two?

Noon taps the image of one of the girls.

                              MIA (CONT'D)
     The one on the right?

Noon shakes her head 'yes' and is about to walk away.

Mia looks down the alley at an overweight white getting head in a doorway.

Noon looks at the photo again.

                                  NOON
     She look like girl I meet on bus.

                                   MIA
     When?

                                  NOON
     Maybe six months ago. Very pretty girl.

Mia reacts with some enthusiasm.

                          MIA
     Where was the bus going?

                          NOON
     You don't look Chinese?

                          MIA
     Vietnamese.

                          NOON
     First, a trip to Paris, a lie. Change of plan. Then, say they
     taking us to a shelter. Another lie.

                          MIA
     Do you remember her name?

                          NOON
     Don't remember. Maybe like Angie. Only together for a short time.
     But all girls get new names. Make us into different girls. Family
     name history. Don't know what happened to her. We both tried to
     escape. In river. I got away.

Noon pulls out a mirror and looks at herself.

                          NOON (CONT'D)
     You want big drama story? Make you feel worse not better.

Noon turns back towards Mia, now only a few inches away from her face.

Noon takes her hand and gently traces the side of Mia's face and lips.

                          NOON (CONT'D)

     No shelter. Driver made his own deal. We taken to village near
     ocean. I been to places like that before. Army base few k's away.

     Villages sometimes worse then Patpong. They treat us like cattle.
     Fifteen to twenty farang a day. You open your mouth and spread your
     legs so they at least feed you and don't beat you. They must have
     caught her when we try to run. One soldier had eye on her. Maybe
     good, maybe bad. He think he movie star or something.

Noon shrugs her shoulders.

                          NOON (CONT'D)
     I can swim. I lucky one.

Mia stands speechless. Noon starts to walk away.

                              NOON (CONT'D)
          Girls here same story. Picked up, stolen or sold. Many poor peasant
          girls. Better for family they gone. Sometimes they send money home
          They bring them here and soon make look like candy, dessert.

Noon turns and holds out her hand.

                              NOON (CONT'D)
          I talk to you long time.

Mia hands her additional money.

                              NOON (CONT'D)
          This girl you looking for... She very lucky girl. Some one take
          care of the pretty girls. Average like me end up here. Never see
          her here... Never.

Noon gently bows, puts on her head phones, and disappears down a side street.

INT. PINK CHERRY - FOLLOWING MOURNING

Mia sits at a table alone.

Mia sees Kit approaching through the mirror behind the bar.

                              MIA

               I was expecting you last night.

                              KIT

                It's been over six years.

               Did you ever tell him the truth?

Mia shakes her head 'no' while Kit looks into the mirror at Jimme and Joy at
the bar.

                              KIT (CONT'D)
          Why didn't you answer any of my e-mails?

                              MIA
          I need a cup of coffee.

                              KIT
          The questions you have been asking, taking photos, this has to
          stop.

Mia pops a few pills taken from her jacket pocket. Kit nods toward Jade.

Mia looks frustrated as she takes a sip of coffee. Kit leans towards her.

                              KIT (CONT'D)
          If you want to talk to someone... talk to me.

Moments later.

Mia stares elusively out the club window.

                              MIA
          Have you ever thought what it would have been like if we had stayed
          in 'Nam?

                              KIT

                    No.

In a faded mirror, Mia sees Alan's reflection as he enters the
club.

                              KIT

                    Fuck me!

Alan enters, donning Ray Bans, a Yankee cap, a Ramones T-shirt and
a three day old beard. There eyes meet.

                              KIT
          What in hell is he doing here?

                              MIA
          Not the time or the place.

Mia grimaces as Alan's hand caresses her shoulder.

                              ALAN
          I see you're feeling better.

With her eyes, Mia motions for Alan to sit. Alan stares at Kit suspiciously.

                              KIT
          Good morning.

Kit rises from his chair, intending to shake hands. Alan nods and sits down.

                              ALAN
          So you went from a cop servicing pimps to a pimp servicing cops?

                              KIT
          I own a nightclub.

Kit looks back and sees that Jimme is heading toward the table.

Jimme now stands to the side of Kit.

                            JIMME
          My dear Mr. Lee, who are these two lovely people?

Alan looks into the cup to see what Mia is drinking.

                             KIT
          This is my sister, Mia, and her husband, Alan.

Jimme nods and smiles.

                            JIMME
          Do not want to bother you, but just wanted to remind you of the
          business get together we have planned for next week. Have you
          spoken with Mr. Ford?

Kit looks up at Jimme.

                             KIT
          On my calendar. Everything will be ready. Actually, meeting with
          Mr. Ford later tonight.

Jimme smiles and looks out toward the entrance of the restaurant. Noon sits at
the far end of the bar.

Jimme smiles and pats Kit on the shoulder.

                            JIMME
          Great. If you have a chance you two should stop into my place. Just
          around the corner. Nine Lives Club. We actually have some of the
          best Thai food in Patpong... and some lovely ladies.

Mia and Alan smile as Jimme turns and heads back toward the bar.

                            ALAN
          Kit, just love the club. Did they throw you off the force, or did
          you decide running your own skin joint was a better income than
          taking bribes from pimps and drug lords?

Kit watches as Jimme leaves the restaurant with Joy.

                        ALAN (CONT'D)
          Is that clown one of your pimps or some want-to-be warlord?

Kit rises from the table and leans toward Mia.

                              KIT
          I will be by later to say goodbye... before you go back home.

Mia looks at Kit with a troubled smile and gathers her belongings, then turns
around to look over the working girls.

Kit stakes a few steps toward Alan and is now in his face.

                         KIT (SOFTLY) (CONT'D)
          If I see you within ten feet of my nightclub again, I will have
          your sorry ass arrested or maybe tell one of my buddies that you
          love sky diving, a couple hundred feet above the fucking ocean...

Kit turns and looks at Mia then back at Alan.

                           KIT (CONT'D)
          If you care anything about her... get her the fuck out of here. You
          saved her life once... time to save it again.

Kit walks away. Alan follows him with his eyes as Mia walks back to Alan.

                              ALAN
          Ever think about what would have happened to you if I had left you
          and your asshole brother in Saigon?

Mia steps forward with a bitter smile on her face. A momentary face-off.

                              MIA
          Of all the cock I was paid to fuck and suck in Saigon, how the
          fuck did I end up with you?

Mia reaches up and grabs Alan by the throat.

                           MIA (CONT'D)
          I'm going to say it one more time. We are no longer partners,
          lovers, or friends. Stay out of my fucking life!

MOMENTS LATER

Alan sits alone sipping the rest of Mia's coffee. A look of sad anger fills his
face.

INT. MIA'S HOTEL ROOM - LATER THAT NIGHT

The room is bare. A creaking fan blows air against a blouse thrown over a
chair. A jug of water and an empty bottle of liquor stand on a small table next
to the bed.

Mia pops open a bottle of pills, swallowing a couple.

She staggers toward a small table, grabbing the house phone.

                              MIA
          I know it is three o'clock in the morning. All I want is a drink.
          One fucking drink!

Mia turns and looks at her reflection in the mirror. She makes the clothes she
is wearing a little more revealing. She fluffs her hair.

                              MIA (CONT'D)
                            (loudly)
          I do not have a real husband! He was an escape route. My way out
          of hell.

She turns, opens the door and walks out into the hotel corridor.

She KNOCKS on a room door. No answer.

She POUNDS on another door. An old man opens the door.

                              MIA (CONT'D)
          Do you have anything to drink?

He shakes his head and closes the door.

Another door opens. An INDIAN MALE in his 60s steps out.

                              OLD MAN
          It is three o'clock in the morning.

Mia steps towards him, trying to play seductive. She flashes him, then pulls
her robe closed.

                              MIA
          Sweetheart, you alone? We could have a few drinks and who knows...

                              OLD MAN
          I'm going to call security.

                              MIA
          Fuck! All I want is something to drink!

He slams the door shut.

                              MIA (CONT'D)
          Ha Mahatma... Terrific, call security. When they come up, tell them
          to bring me a bottle of Jack Daniels!

A male figure approaches from behind her.

She stops at another door and is about to pound again.

Kit grabs Mia from behind, holding her firmly like he's escorting a felon to their cell.

Hotel employees approach. Kit motions that everything is under control.

INT. MIA'S ROOM - MOMENTS LATER

Mia staggers across the room, knocking over a chair. She moves to the closet and rips clothes off hangers.

> MIA
>
> Leave me the fuck alone! Who the fuck do you think you are? I don't see you for six years and all of a sudden you think you can become a part of my life! You want to fuck like old times?

Kit stares at the distant wall of photographs.

> MIA (CONT'D)
>
> Why did you let me marry that asshole? Why didn't you come for me?

Kit takes a few steps closer to the wall of photos.

> MIA (CONT'D)
>
> Guess I'm the next fucking Diane Arbus.

Mia collapses onto the bed.

> KIT
>
> People are beginning to ask questions. Many of the girls don't want people to know they're here. Trafficking is not a word that is used in Patpong. Prostitution is legal in Bangkok.

> MIA
>
> Prostitution may be legal in Bangkok, but kidnapping and buying and selling human beings is not.

Kit sits on the chair next to her and gently strokes her back and shoulders.

> KIT
>
> I'll stay until you go to sleep.

> MIA
>
> I can't fucking sleep.

Mia attempts to smile to stop herself from crying.

She leans forward and kisses Kit on the lips. Kit takes her hand. She freezes as their eyes meet.

Mia picks up the empty bottle of scotch. KNOCK at the door.

A young waiter enters carrying a tray with coffee and biscuits. He puts it down
on the table and leaves.

                              KIT

     Drink it!

Reluctantly, she takes a sip.

Kit gets up and puts on his jacket

                         KIT (CONT'D)
          You could have stayed with me in Bangkok.

                         MIA
          An eighteen-year-old girl with no money, no connections, nothing.
          You know what I did to survive in Saigon. He was willing to forget.

Kit leans forward and kisses her.

Mia steps away and walks toward the mirror.

                         MIA (CONT'D)
          He saved our lives. He got us both out of Saigon.

Looking at herself in the mirror.

                         MIA (CONT'D)
          I think once I was actually trying to love him.

Mia turns around and walks back toward Kit.

                         MIA (CONT'D)
          Too bad he turned out to be such a dick.

Mia embraces and kisses Kit like there is no tomorrow.

MOMENTS LATER

Kit sits in a wicker chair across from Mia's bed. He watches a news broadcast
on the television. President Clinton doing his "I did not have sex with Monica
Lewinsky" translated in Thai on the screen.

Mia comes in from the terrace.

                              KIT
          How did you convince him to allow me to get on that helicopter?

                                  MIA
          I told him that if my brother could not come with me I was staying
          in Saigon.

                                  KIT
          What would you have done if he had said no, or found out we were
          lovers... that I am not your brother?

                                  MIA
          He didn't.

Mia pops open a bottle of pills, downing a couple with what is left of a bottle
of water.

                                  KIT
          What's the medication?

                                  MIA
          Something that helps put a smile on my face.

Kit looks at a pile of photos on the floor.

                                  KIT
          The photographs?

Kit picks up the photo that she carries around with her. Mia heads toward the
window.

                                  MIA
          Keith told me you work both sides of what he calls the 'highway'?
          You own a nightclub called the Pink Cherry. You employ young
          women who are paid to be eye candy, and for the right price they
          can...

                                  KIT
          Good clubs and bad clubs. This keeps a roof over their heads and
          food in their stomachs.

Kit begins to button his shirt.

                                  MIA
          I would like to interview some of your girls. No names. Let the
          girls tell their own stories.

                                  KIT
          So you can get yourself or one of these girls killed?

Kit gets up and walks toward the door.

                                        MIA
          With or without you, I will find her.

Mia turns and walks towards him. They embrace.

Kit hesitates as Mia turns and heads toward the bathroom.

                                   MIA (CONT'D)
          I need to freshen up.

Kit tosses his jacket on the bed and flips through 20 copies of the *Newsweek*
photo. He takes one and puts the photograph in his jacket pocket.

INT. BATHROOM - MOMENTS LATER - SHOWER

Mia rests in a squat position, as water flowing from the shower caresses her
naked body.

Kit comes into the bathroom and gets undressed.

                                        MIA
          Why did it take me so long to have a child? We had stopped trying.
          I was fucking 38-years-old.

Kit is about to say something but doesn't.

The wet stone floor is punctuated with frangipani petals as Mia squats on the
tile floor gently sobbing. Kit bends down behind her and holds her in his arms.

Mia, with her fingers, gently moves a number of flower petals over the wet
stone shower floor.

FLASHBACK:

INT. BANGKOK - HOTEL RESTAURANT - DAY - EIGHT YEARS AGO

Mia, her 12-year-old daughter ASIA, and Alan sit alongside a pool having a late
breakfast.

Alan sips his coffee.

Asia, her long black hair in braids sits next to Mia, looking at a book.

                                       ASIA
          I'm bored.

                                        MIA
          Please, honey, your father and I are trying to have a conversation.

Asia throws the book to the ground. Mia gives her a hard stare.

                              ASIA
          This is not fun.

                              MIA
          I had lunch with Keith Ford from the State Department.

                              ALAN
          Did he hit on you again?

                              MIA
          I'm too old for him. Last time I saw him at a party he was with
          something half his age. Obviously paid for by good old Uncle Sam.

                              ALAN
          The idea was to take some time off.

                              MIA
          Word is out that soldiers have begun an ethnic cleansing in Darfur.

                              ALAN
          I don't think this is the time or that is the place for you to take
          off again. Why should we give a damn about what happens in some
          fucking God-forsaken shit-hole in Africa? You haven't seen your
          brother in twelve years.

Mia looks at him, as if wanting him and discarding him were synonymous.

                              MIA
          Two weeks is enough.

EXT. OTHER SIDE OF POOL - SAME

Asia walks along the side of the pool. A small dog comes out from behind some
potted palms. Asia bends down and plays with the dog.

A young attractive Asian woman comes to fetch the dog. Asia and the woman
exchange a smile and a brief conversation. The three of them disappear on the
other side of the potted palms.

POOL SIDE

                              MIA
          He knows where I am, where we lived. It's not just a one way
          street.

Mia gets up from the table, seemingly some what distracted, strokes her hair,
adjusts her skirt, and turns around.

                              MIA (CONT'D)
          Where in hell did she go?

Mia speaks with one of the attendants, who shakes his head no.

                              MIA (CONT'D)
          She can't swim.

                              ALAN
          I'll check the pool.

POOL AREA - SAME

Alan looks at the crystal blue water and a few swimmers.

Mia continues looking along the perimeter of the court yard. No one has seen her.

Mia goes to the snack bar. A young WAITRESS approaches.

                              WAITRESS
          Your daughter was walking with a pretty woman and a small dog.

The waitress points to the crowded side street.

Mia walks out into the middle of the street as she dials her cell phone.

                              MIA
          Kit!

INT. BATHROOM - MOMENTS LATER - REAL TIME

Water caresses Mia and Kit as they stand in a naked embrace in the shower.

                              KIT
          Tomorrow I'll give the photo to someone I trust with the police.

EXT. SILOM ROAD - LATER SAME DAY

Alan walks the streets of the infamous red light district.

A number of young girls hang out on the staircase of the Nine Lives Club.

Fake MTV smiles and painted eyes caress Alan.

INT. BAR - CONTINUOUS

Alan sits at the bar as three young girls pole dance a few feet away.

Mirror directly behind dancing girls.

Alan sees the reflection in the mirror of Jimme as he enters the nightclub. Jimme Stops and says something to Joy then leaves.

A number of girls approach Alan. Joy, carrying a drink, waves the others off.

                              JOY
     May I sit here?

No response from Alan as he continues to watch the pole dancers and Sunglasses.

                         JOY (CONT'D)
     What can I help you with tonight?

Alan takes out some bills. Joy seems nervous.

Alan watches as Jimme talks with another man in the far corner of the
nightclub. Joy follows Alan's gaze.

                              ALAN
     What can you tell me about that man?

                              JOY
     Much better if we talk in private.

Alan hesitates.

Joy picks up Alan's drink and takes his hand. Joy and Jimme exchange a glance.

MOMENTS LATER

Alan and Joy climb a bamboo staircase. Joy opens one of the rooms. Two girls
and an older man in bed. She closes the door.

MOANING can be heard from another room.

Joy takes a key and opens the door to the last room on the left.

Joy takes his hand and walks Alan toward the bed. Alan sits at the end of the
bed.

                              ALAN
     I thought we were just talking?

Joy takes out a cigarette, lights it, and offers one to Alan. Alan shakes his
head no.

Joy takes off her top.

                              JOY
                         (whispering)
     We can talk but we have to fuck.

Joy nods toward a camera in the corner ceiling of the room. Joy turns away from
the camera and drops her skirt.

                              JOY (CONT'D)
    The cameras make sure no one gets hurt or takes money and hides
    it. Occasionally depending on who the John is they use the film to
    blackmail him.

Naked, Joy walks toward the bathroom.

                              JOY (CONT'D)
    Let me freshen up.

Alan looks around the room. He leans over and opens a drawer in the night
stand. A gun.

Joy exits the bathroom wrapped in a towel.

Joy takes his hand and rubs it between her legs.

                              ALAN
    The gun?

Joy smiles, opens the drawer and puts the gun to the side of his head. CLICK,
CLICK. Alan jumps back.

                              JOY
    Some assholes after shooting off their gun decide, don't want
    to pay, or they play to rough. Then we show them we have bigger,
    sexier gun. Some old timers piss in the bed. I then take all the
    money they have on them with gun pointed at their now limp gun.

Joy removes a condom from a small night stand.

Joy straddles Alan locating herself properly over his groin. She gently begins
to rock back and forth.

Alan is now aroused. Joy leans down toward Alan's face. He tries to kiss her on
the lips.

                              JOY (CONT'D)
    No lips. Kissing lips is for people you care about, you love. The
    girls kiss with their pussies. I make love to your cock not you.

She moves closer kissing his cheeks and ear.

                        JOY (WHISPER) (CONT'D)
    Your wife is asking for trouble. People looking for daughters go
    home after a threat they will only hear once, or often don't make
    it home at all.

Joy pulls away. Alan has cum.

Now standing, Joy wipes the inside of her thighs with the sheet.

                              JOY (CONT'D)
          Go rinse off.

Joy firmly nods toward the bathroom.

INT. BATHROOM - CONTINUOUS

Alan stands at the urinal then goes to the sink to wash his hands.

                              JIMME (OC)
          So how do you like our lovely city?

Alan looks up at the mirror and Jimme's reflection. Jimme smiles and takes a
few steps toward Alan.

                              JIMME (CONT'D)
          Listen carefully. The business men who run these establishments
          do not like people, especially 'snoop dog' westerners going into
          clubs, taking pictures, asking questions, looking for missing
          girls. Very, very bad for business.

Alan says nothing.

                              JIMME (CONT'D)
          Another language that you would prefer or would you like me to
          speak louder.

Jimme straightens his shirt and fixes his hair in the mirror.

                              JIMME (CONT'D)
          I can't even imagine what it would be like to lose a child. It
          brings tears to my eyes. But from the look of things, she's dead,
          gone, did an unfortunate adiós.

Alan turns and grabs Jimme by the throat. They exchange a few blows.

Jimme breaks free and with a hard shot to the side of the head knocks Alan
against the wall.

A young Thai male holds Alan in tow.

                              JIMME (CONT'D)
          There was really no reason for this to get physical.

Jimme hits Alan hard in the stomach, followed by a few blows to the head.

Alan lies on the tile floor bleeding from the mouth.

Jimme again fixes his hair in the mirror as the young Thai puts a gun to Alan's head.

Joy enters the bathroom.

                              JIMME (CONT'D)
What's the word you Americans use as an excuse to not feel heartache?

Jimme looks down at Alan.

                              JIMME (CONT'D)
Oh, yes. It's time for you and that lovely MLTF of yours to find...
closure. You have twenty-four hours.

Jimme steps toward Noon and kisses her on the check

Joy looks down at Alan and shakes her head no. Jimme grabs her by the arm as
they exit the bathroom. Alan remains seated on the floor.

EXT. BANGKOK NEIGHBORHOOD MARKET - TWO DAYS LATER - NIGHT

Mia and Kit leave a restaurant and roam the crowded stands and booths that
border Patpong. A group of Western tourist's watch a snake charmer toy with a
cobra.

Kit watches a plasma screen from a store window.

                    INDIAN ANCHORWOMAN (ENGLISH SUB - TITLES)
The rash of hotel robberies continues. Over the past two weeks
seventeen robberies have occurred in six major hotels.

Kit answers his cell phone.

                              KIT
          Yes.

Kit steps out of the way of pedestrian traffic.

TELEPHONE

                              KEITH
          The event.

                              KIT
          What about it?

                              KEITH
Our new Japanese friends. They want the new models, no retreads or
test drives.

Kit watches as Mia does some window shopping.

                              KEITH (CONT'D)
She and her ex seem to have patched things up. Our friend had a
meeting with her ex. Went well. He got the message. I left plane
tickets for them at the hotel.

The phone goes dead.

Mia stops and looks at her reflection in the window store glass as Kit becomes part of the refection.

                              KIT
          I'll drop you off at the hotel. I'll be back later.

                              MIA.
          No, I'm fine. I'll get a taxi.

Kit steps out into the street and stops a taxi.

The taxi window slowly goes down as Kit opens the rear door.

                              KIT
          Oberoi Hotel... When were you going to tell me you were leaving?

Mia looks surprised.

                              MIA
          Not until I find her. Alan can leave anytime he wants.

Mia gives Kit a kiss.

Mia watches as Kit crosses the street and gets in a black Range Rover. Jade is driving. The Range Rover pulls away.

INT. TAXI - SAME

The driver looks in his rear view mirror.

                              DRIVER
          Oberoi... Get you there very fast.

Mia stares blankly out the window.

                              MIA
          No... Follow them.

EXT. BANGKOK DOCK - LATER THAT NIGHT

The black Range Rover pulls up alongside a dock area lined with rows of containers.

EXT. DOCK - CONTINUOUS

A few yards away Keith stands looking up at a gorgeous night sky.

Kit and Jade step out the car and walk toward Keith. Keith turns toward Kit and lights a cigarette.

                              KEITH
          The nights are so beautiful after the rain washes away our dirty
          halo.

Jade walks past Keith as if he is invisible.

                              KEITH (CONT'D)
          We did not want Jimme to get involved.

Jade watches as one of the cranes circles to pluck a container off the deck of
a freighter.

                              KEITH (CONT'D)
          I don't want anyone to get killed.

Keith tosses the cigarette.

                              KEITH
          He's making a deal with the Japanese outfit out of Tokyo.

DOCK - SAME

Jade looks at her reflection in the water. The container CLANKS against the
dock.

                              KEITH
          Some very big players. Word is they gross about $1.8 million a year
          via pussy. They're tired of getting their hands dirty. So Jimme is
          now the middle man, and you're their travel agent. No runaways,
          drug addicts, or sex-club wash-outs. Clean and fresh. None older
          than 18. Over the next month, he needs 250 girls.

                              KIT
          Two months ago we made two shipments to Uzbekistan of over thirty
          girls. Didn't happen. Why?

                              KEITH
          A screw up. Shit happens.

                              KIT
          The money could be bullshit. They get nothing until...

Jade now stands a few feet away.

                              KEITH
          I've set this deal up a little differently. The deposit is going to
          be in cash.

                              JADE
          Cash?

                              KEITH
          250,000, in Euros.

Jade looks at Kit.

                              JADE
          Think of what you could do with that kind of money.

Keith looks at Kit as they walk toward the container.

                              KIT
          The plan was to close these assholes down.

Keith steps closer to Kit.

                              KEITH
          We split the cash, and take out the Japanese bag men at the same
          time. Make it look like Jimme did it.

CONTAINER - SAME

Kit steps back a few feet seemingly disgusted with the situation.

                              KEITH
          Then I'm out of here... Getting too old for this shit.

Both men look at the container.

                              KIT
          Where's the fucking bus?

EXT. YARD AREA - SAME

A taxi slowly pulls up outside the dock area.

INTERIOR TAXI - CONTINUOUS

                              MIA
          Turn off your head lights and wait.

EXT. SIDE OF CONTAINER - SAME

Kit looks at a pair of eyes peeking out one of the vent holes on the side of
the container.

TAXI - SAME

Mia gets out of the taxi as a school bus slowly pulls into the lot.

SCHOOL BUS - CONTINUOUS

Mookie climbs out of the bus as Keith approaches.

                              KEITH
          Where the fuck have you been?

                              MOOKIE
          Argentina 2, Spain 1.

Another young male Thai begins cutting the links on the door of the container
as Jade watches.

The container door is slowly pulled open.

Illuminated by the over head harbor lights, two frightened girls stand at the
open door of the container.

Additional girls sit or rest on thirty to forty sleeping bags and a few soiled
mattresses. A porta-san (portable toilet) at the end of the interior. Empty
plastic bottles, trash and some rotten fruit litter the floor.

Jade back steps from the open door.

                              JADE
          Smells like a fucking latrine.

The derelict-looking girls slowly exit the container. Keith turns and looks at
Mia as she approaches.

                              KEITH
          Fuck me!

Mia confronts the two men.

                              MIA
          Are they being rescued or sold?

                              KIT
          These girls are on their way to a shelter.

                              MIA
          Right, and Lewinsky didn't give Clinton head.

Sweeping car head lights sweep the dock.

Mia stops and looks back at the entrance to the port as a police vehicle pulls
into the yard, blocking the gate.

                              MIA (CONT'D)
          Are they here to help or...

Mia removes her camera from her bag and takes a few photos of the girls.

                         KEITH
          What the fuck do you think you are doing?

Keith gives Kit a stare and shakes his head no. Jade walks toward the girls.

                         JADE
          Anyone speak Thai?

No one answers as Mia looks at the girls again then back at Kit.

Mia walks toward the cluster of girls.

MIA (SPEAKS IN VIETNAMESE)

Your trip is over. You will be given clean clothes, a shower, and a good meal.

Jade motions for the girls to head toward the bus.

                         MIA (CONT'D)
          A whole new concept of boat people. This is repulsive.

Keith now stands next to Mia.

                         KEITH
          You have no idea what we do, what your fucking brother does. Only
          way to try and be the good guys is to be part of the bad guys
          game. Try to stop them in the red zone.

                         MIA
          Your football metaphor sucks.

Kit has already left the conversation and walks towards Mookie.

PARKING AREA - CONTINUOUS

                         KIT
          Your story about the bus from the airport being high-jacked is
          probably bullshit.

Mookie shows him the bruise on his arms and face. Mia steps past Kit and closer
to Mookie.

                         KIT (CONT'D)
          Tell Mr. Jimme that your high-jacking of that bus, has got a woman
          police officer, one of the good ones, really pissed of.

Mia now stands a foot away from Mookie, face-to-face.

                              MIA
          And where did you find this piece of road kill?

Mookie's nostrils flare as he glares at Mia.

Kit steps between them as Mia turns her attention back toward the girls.

                              KIT
          Any of these girls gets touched and the next time you take a pee
          you will be taking it from a slit between your fucking legs.

Kit walks closer to Mookie so Mia can not hear.

                         KIT (CONT'D)
          Word to remember: cherry. This is like fresh fruit from the market.

Kit turns and walks toward Mia. Mookie flips them the finger.

Mia steps forward as Kit approaches.

                              MIA
          When are you going to get tired of being these cock-suckers black
          market travel agent?

Mia steps away and heads toward the taxi.

Kit watches as the last of the girls gets on the bus.

Head lights illuminate the parking lot as Mia's taxi pulls away.

BUS - SAME

Kit slowly walks toward the now full bus. Jade steps down from the bus.

                              JADE
          What are we doing?

                              KIT
          Get them cleaned-up, feed them. They need to be ready for tomorrow
          night

INT. REAR SEAT OF LIMO - SAME

Keith looks at his refection in the mirror as he pulls out his cellphone and
the limo slowly leaves the yard.

                             KEITH
          Laszlo, Keith Ford. (Russian) Can you meet me for breakfast
          tomorrow? Want to finalize our business arrangement and I need
          your expertise on a personal matter.

Great. The Oberoi at nine o'clock.

INT. HOTEL ROOM - FOLLOWING MORNING

Mia stands in front of a mirror toweling her hair dry. Her cell phone rings.

                    MIA
          Yes. Why? I don't think continuing this is a good idea. It was
          easier when you were my brother... What? Tomorrow morning. I can
          talk with them? No photos?...OK, OK, I got it no photographs. What
          time? I'll meet you down stairs.

EXT. PATPONG - LATE NIGHT

The brightly-lit streets are filled with a United Nations of middle=aged males,
teenage male Thais, food stalls, girls, a few couples, and Mia.

Mia dodges a variety of cycles, carts and mostly male tourists as she crosses
the street.

Mia stops and concentrates on a large staircase that leads to a double-neon-
lit, open double door.

A group of young girls dance to the beat of rock music.

Mia stands to the side of the staircase, focuses and begins to take photos.

Mia continues her walk. As she takes a picture of a young male and two girls,
one with a boa, the young male stops in stride giving her a cold stare.

Mia smiles.

                    MIA (THAI)
          Nice snake.

She walks past them.

INT. NINE LIVES CLUB - MOMENTS LATER

Jimmie sits at bar with laptop. He scrolls. Types in Mia's name. Images pop up.
Cover photo for book. *Mia Douglas: Destination Danger, Photographs*. He quickly
flips through a few.

Mia enters behind him and heads towards the bar. Mia buys a drink.

The club floor is lined with tables circling small stages. On each stage a girl
half-dressed or completely nude suggestively dances or performs some kind of
erotic act.

Jimme sits alone in the corner of the bar area.

Mia removes her camera and begins to take photos of the girls.

Jimme gets up, drink in hand, and walks like a predator toward Mia.

                          JIMME
          So, we meet again.

Mia sips from her drink as Jimme sits across from her.

                          JIMME (CONT'D)
          Where is your husband?

Mia finishes sips her drink.

                          MIA
          He was supposed to meet me here.

Jimme notices the camera between her legs.

                          JIMME (CONT'D)
          I guess that is one way to take him to the cleaners.

A lovely bartender puts a drink down on the bar.

                          JIMME (CONT'D)
          Thank you, my dear.

                          MIA

          Cleaners?

                          JIMME
          Your husband. My bad joke. Last night your husband dropped by.
          Thought he came for the food... but instead he fucked one of my top
          girls. I introduced myself again to him when he was done. Told him
          I have a ten-minute video.

                          MIA
          I could care less what he does. We are getting a divorce. Most men
          come to Bangkok to fuck... not to eat Thai food.

Jimme smiles and leans closer.

                          JIMME
          I went online. Saw your work. You are very good photojournalist.
          You must be brave to go to all those dangerous places.

DISTANT TABLE - SAME

To their left a middle-aged male is pulled from his chair by two young men and
roughly escorted to the exit.

                              JIMME (CONT'D)
          Some of our gentleman don't understand that you can't touch the
          merchandise.

                                 MIA
          I guess you have different rules for the floor.

Mia looks up at the catwalk above them and the numerous numbered doors.

                              MIA (CONT'D)
          How old are those girls?

Jimme waves to a table of three men who leave with three of the girls.

                                JIMME
          Old enough to know they have a roof over their head and food in
          their bellies.

Mia downs the rest of her drink and gives him a look that fires bullets.

                                 MIA
          So all of these club owners, pimps, kidnappers, traffickers are
          just good Samaritans? Bullshit.

Mia smiles an awkward smile as she leaves some baht on the counter

Jimme pushes the money back to Mia.

                                JIMME
          You ask way too many questions.

                                 MIA
          In today's world, hard to find an honest truthful answer. Fake
          news.

Jimme downs his drink.

                                JIMME
          This is not fake news. Your dickhead husband will be telling you
          that his vacation have been shortened. He will be out of here by
          weekend. (SOFTLY) And if I were you... I would take that tight
          little ass and that honest to God camera of yours and leave with
          him. That camera and where you're pointing it... like my road-kill
          friend, (HE LAUGHS) although accurate... That comment really pissed
          him off, to some can very easily end up a death sentence. No Fox
          News bullshit..

          That's truth and its consequences.

Jimme adjusts his glasses, sits straight, and offers Mia his Hollywood smile.

Mia slides off the stool and heads toward the door.

                    JIMME (CONT'D)
     When you say goodbye to your lovely brother, please tell him
     we need to talk. Need to make sure those lovely, about-to-bloom
     flowers... I think that they from your homeland... will be ready
     for tomorrow night.

Mia exits as Jimme stares suggestively at one of his young bouncers. He nods
his head in Mia's direction then turns his attention back to the girl at the
bar.

The girl who had been dancing for the men that were earlier thrown out of the
club removes a number of baht from her shorts and gives it to Jimme.

Exiting, Mia takes her camera, focusing on Jimme and the young man now standing
next to him. Mia zooms in. CLICK, CLICK.

Jimme can see Mia's refection in the mirror behind the bar. Jimme smiles and
waves at her. Mia gives him the finger.

EXT. STREET - MINUTES LATER

Mia walks past a number of food carts, stops, and purchases a bottle of water.

Mia turns and heads down a side street. Across the street two young males step
out from an alleyway. They block her from passing, knock her to the pavement,
kick at her and rough her up.

Two YOUNG WHITE MEN exit one of the clubs on the street. They see what's going
on, yell, and run toward the fallen Mia.

The hoods take Mia's bag and camera and flee.

Mia pulls herself to her feet. She looks at a bruise on her arm and tastes the
blood from her mouth as the two white men are at he side. Mia walks away in the
protection of the two men.

INT. HOTEL RESTAURANT - FOLLOWING MORNING

Keith sits at a table with two middle-aged EASTERN EUROPEAN MEN.

A young Thai girl places food in front of the three men.

                    KEITH
     Thank you, sweetheart.

He winks at the waitress and smiles at the two men.

                    KEITH (RUSSIAN) (CONT'D)
     I know you are here to solve a problem. First, I have the girls.
     Second, you will get the girls. Third, your payback has changed a
     little.

The two men look at each other as the older one nods.

                              OLDER MAN
          We will soon deal with the travel agent and his faggot, want-to-be
          soldier partner.

Keith smiles and nods his head yes.

                              KEITH
          Yes, I can't wait. First, there is someone else that needs to be
          removed from the storyboard.

Keith takes a photo from his pocket and places it in front of the two men.

                              OLDER MAN
What she have to do with this?

Keith smiles and continues eating. It is a photo of Mia and Alan.

                              KEITH
          She is an American, a journalist. She is the sister of your travel
          agent. They make fucking books about her. She is all over fucking
          Google. She has been taking photos: the girls, the clubs, me, and
          you. For all I know, she also has photos of your boss.

          The bitch loves tragedy. (Keith leans forward.) She is the fucking
          dark side.

Keith laughs at a joke he knows they did not get. The two hoods look at each other.

                              KEITH (CONT'D)
          I remember how quickly you took care of that removal a few months
          ago in Beijing. That was between me and you... same here.

The younger man nods.

                              KEITH (CONT'D)
          The Oberoi. There have been a shitload of hotel robberies.

Keith slides a sealed envelope across the table.

                              KEITH (CONT'D)
          Five thousand now, five when she is yesterday's news.

                              OLDER HOOD
What about him?

                              KEITH
          Both of them... and make sure you get her fucking laptop. Bring me
          the laptop.

EXT. STREET - SAME MORNING

Mia stands in front of an office directory: "Overseas Placements Fourth Floor."
A GUARD watches TV.

Mia climbs the stairs to the fourth floor.

INT. OFFICE - SAME

Jade, in casual dress, is getting ready to leave the office. Jade gets up from
the desk and lets Mia in.

                              JADE
          Something that I can help you with?

                              MIA
          I was looking for my brother.

                              JADE (CONT'D)
          Not sure where he is.

Mia slowly patrols the office looking at the photographs on the walls. Photos of
Kit with several groups of teenage females.

                              MIA
          All of these?

                              JADE
          Yes. They have all part of Mr. Lee's relocations.

                              MIA
          My brother is a very busy man.

Mia walks toward Jade at her desk and looks at a photo.

Jade looks at the photograph of a younger image of herself standing next to Kit.

                              JADE
          I was sold by my father to the owner of a KTV bar. When I met Kit,
          I was about to be sold again to the owner of a sneaker company.
          Kit saved my life.

Jade seems flustered and not sure what to say or do.

                              JADE (CONT'D)
          That business, sometimes it can be to some a blessing, an actual
          job, a roof over your head, food in your belly. Sometimes, most of
          time, a horror a nightmare that you didn't plan for. Much of the
          time it is pieces of both.

Mia looks around they office not knowing what to do next.

                         JADE (CONT'D)
          Kit told me about the kidnapping of your daughter.

Mia gives Jade a questionable stare.

                         JADE (CONT'D)
             It's fucking hot in here.

Jade gets up and goes to the window lifting it open a few inches.

                         JADE (CONT'D)
          I have to pee.

Bathroom door closes. Mia hurries to the file cabinets, looks through files,
and some additional photos. Takes nothing. Walks to the desk, looks at the
computer, almost touches it, picks up the bus photo, looks at the open window.
and exits.

Jade comes out of the bathroom, picks up her coat, looks at the window then her
desk, flips the lights off and leaves the office.

EXT. ALLY - FIRE ESCAPE - THAT NIGHT

Mia moves cautiously through a tight alley. Garbage cans, cats, fire escape.

Mia begins climbing a fire escape. Mia at window that has been left open.

Mia pulls window open and enters the space. With light from cell phone, she
scans the room.

Jade's desk, the computer has been left on.

Mia sits. She views photographs similar to head shots: Asian, Caucasian, Slavic,
African. Some of the groups are indicated by countries: Cambodia, India, Nepal,
and Vietnam.

With her other hand, Mia fumbles through her bag, finally removing a memory stick.

Inserting the device she begins to pull up additional files.

NOISE from the hallway.

MINUTES LATER

Mia turns and looks out the window and fire escape.

                         MIA
          Come on, come on.

The office door opens.

Mia falls flat onto the fire escape.

INT. OFFICE - SAME

A OLDER THAI WOMAN with cleaning gear turns on the office lights and enters the room.

Mia hails a taxi. The taxi turns around and heads down the street and into the heart of Bangkok.

INT. RESTAURANT - THAT MORNING

Mia enters the restaurant looking like she did the night before. She goes to the table and pours herself a cup of coffee, eats a strip of bacon, scoops some fruit into a bowl.

She turns to leave and sees Keith sitting in a booth in a fresh suit and tie. He motions for her to join him.

Reluctantly she walks toward Keith's booth.

                    KEITH
          Good morning. Looks like you took on a little more then you...

Keith lights a cigarette and offers one to Mia. Mia looks at some skid-like marks from the fire escape that stain the sleeves of her jacket.

                    KEITH (CONT'D)
          (leans across the table) Sometimes having balls the size of mangoes
          can get you in some nasty shit.

                    MIA
          I always knew that you had a fixation for my imaginary genitalia.

                    KEITH
          Taking photos and asking too many questions. You're lucky you just
          got a couple of fucking bruises.

Mia takes a drag on her cigarette.

                    MIA
          It's now a crime to take pictures and talk to girls on the street?

Mia sips her coffee.

                    KEITH
          Your brother is on the inside lane of a very treacherous highway.
          He's smart, knows the in's and out's and has gained the trust of
          some very, very bad human beings.

Mia begins to eat Keith's croissant.

                              MIA
          Maybe you and my brother should give a little more effort to
          closing these very, very bad human beings down.

                              KEITH
          We try and buy more then we sell. Every once and a while we create
          a fuck-up and shipments are ceased. We set up stings and do close
          some of these motherfuckers down. Play one off the other.

                              MIA
          I don't give a fuck about your macho chess game.

                              KEITH
          This isn't like putting a new face on Times Square. This is
          Bangkok.

                              MIA
          One of these animals you and my brother play your menage-a-trois
          with probably kidnapped my daughter!

                              KEITH
          Right now, you're just his sister. But all someone has to do is
          Google you to find out what you do or did for a living.

                              MIA
          And who is the asshole who helped fuck up what I did for a living?

                              KEITH
          You were told not to set foot near that transition point. Because
          of you three of those women almost didn't make it to that fucking
          helicopter. They would have been killed. Sorry it went bad for
          you on CNN. Sometimes peoples lives are more important then some
          fucking heroic story line.

Mia sips her coffee holding the cup with both hands.

                              KEITH (CONT'D)
          You know sweetheart... If the poor thing is still alive she's
          probably kept up the family tradition.

                              MIA
          Family tradition?

                              KEITH
          If I remember correctly you're the result of your mother's
          relationship with a French soldier. Because of him, your mother no
          longer had to do tricks in the back of some seedy Saigon bar. Your

father vanished. Your mother died and you end up on your knees
with some GI Joe's dick in your mouth while Purple Haze mixes with
some not-so-distant artillery fire.

But you got lucky and were rescued from the shit-hole of post-war
Ho Chi Minh City by one of those GI Joe's you fucked.

Mia can barely control her rage. Keith shakes his head and smiles.

                         KEITH (CONT'D)
     With your genes, and the fact that she can speak English, if
     alive... She probably is applying her trade in one of the better
     skin joints and making big bucks. She can scream in English.

Mia grabs his steak knife and holds it to his throat.

                         MIA
     You say another word about my daughter and I'll--

                         KEITH
     It's time for you to start living life in the real world! She was
     taken over six years ago. For Christ's sake, your precious daughter
     is dead!

Mia sees Kit's SUV pull into the parking lot.

                         MIA
     In case you never figured it out, I'm the cunt who blew the whistle
     on you for trading aid food for sex.

She puts her cigarette out in what's left of his plate of food.

                         MIA (CONT'D)
     I'd pay to watch you take your last stinking breath.

Keith fumes as Mia exits the restaurant.

                         KEITH (V.O.)
     In a few days you will be floating in this lovely harbor as fucking
     chum for the fishes.

Keith downs the rest of his coffee with a sadistic smile.

INT. OLD ORPHANAGE - COUNTRY - BALCONY - SAME AFTERNOON

Kit stands in a hallway surrounded by children.

Mia stands in a yard below speaking with three young girls, girls seen earlier
on the airplane.

A middle-aged AID stands to their left. She translates in English

                         GIRL WITH DYED RED HAIR
          I was stolen on my way to school. They told me if I tried to
          escape they would kill my family.

The other girl, her hair in pigtails, begins to cry. The Aid steps between Mia
and the girls.

                                   AID
          Her mother was killed trying to rescue her. Mr. Kit has been a
          godsend!

Mia watches as Kit talks with one of the older girls showing her a copy of Mia's
photo.

Mia climbs the stairs.

Two girls sit playing a board game. Kit looks at Mia.

                                   MIA
          The good side of your highway.

EXT. ROAD WAY ALONG BEACH - LATER

Kit drives in a black Range Rover. Mia stares out the open passenger window as
they approach a small village.

                                   MIA
          Slow down.

Kit pulls the vehicle up in front of a freshly-painted, one-story, pink
building.

A chicken wire fence capped with barbed wire circles the yard area.

EXT. YARD - SAME

On the other side between the broken strips of fence sit twelve to thirteen
pre-teen and teenage girls.

Mia looks at Kit.

A school.

                                   KIT
          Mia watches as three Caucasian males walk toward the door.

                                   MIA
          And I suppose those clowns are part of the staff? Or are they
          picking up their kids?

                                        KIT
          Stay in the car.

Kit gets out of the car, Mia is already walking toward the fence.

SIDE YARD

Behind the fence, Jimme comes out of a side door holding a rifle. He hastily
moves the girls inside.

FRONT DOOR

Mia KNOCKS then KNOCKS again. Finally the Joy opens the door slightly and
motions for Mia to go away.

                                        MIA
          Excuse me, I'd like to talk to some of the girls.

                                        JOY
          You crazy bitch. Go away!

The door is SLAMMED shut in her face.

Two other MALE TEENAGERS walk slowly toward the car. Kit stands at the side of
the car.

                                        KIT
          Get back into the car!

A young MALE steps out from behind the fence and takes a number of photos of
Mia.

CAR - CONTINUOUS

One of the youths smashes the car head lamps with the butt of his rifle.

Mia gets in the passenger side and closes the door.

Kit is about to go after the teenager, when one of the other teens places the
barrel of his rifle under Kit's chin.

                                   TEENAGER
          You a cop?

Jimme grabs the rifle.

                                     JIMME
          Mr. Lee.

The youth backs away as Kit turns towards Jimme

                              KIT
          The airport is not your territory.

                              JIMME
          Have no idea what you're talking about.

Jimme turns and looks at the car and Mia.

                              JIMME (CONT'D)
          Very pretty sister. You should warn her about the scary side
          streets in Patpong.

INT. PINK BUILDING - SAME

Noon steps away from the window and turns to a large room filled with about ten
GIRLS. Some sit on the floor, some at a table. They are all eating. Pink Floyd
plays in the background.

                              NOON
          That nosy woman.

                              ANGEL
          What woman?

                              NOON
          An American woman. She walk the streets in Patpong with stupid
          photo. Say she doing a story on missing girl. Her daughter.

                              ANGEL
          Photo?

STREET - SAME

Kit takes a few steps closer as Jimme rests the barrel of his rifle against
Kit's chest.

                              JIMME
          I politely warned her and her ex-Nam GI husband that it was time
          to do a sayonara. Remember that song singing Japanese.

                              KIT
          Mookie and you fucked up. The people I sell to did not get there
          merchandise--

                              JIMME
          Stop your bullshit. You already had fucked your buyers. I pay
          Mookie more than you and police do. My new buyer is in town and
          can't wait for our show of perfect fruit from our orchard. No used
          merchandise like most of those girls. Football team... love that.

Kit grabs the barrel of the gun and pushes it away from his chest.

                              KIT
          Tell them they better have cash.

INT. JEEP - SAME

Kit's cell phone rings. Mia lets it ring three times then answers.

                              MIA
          Fuck! Yes. He is indisposed at the moment. Can I take a message?
          Where?... Pandora Hotel... When?... Tomorrow night. Can you confirm
          the time? Midnight. Thank You.

Mia quickly puts the cell phone away as Kit gets into the car.

Kit is agitated as they drive in silence. Kit turns and looks at Mia who
remains silent.

                              KIT
          What about us?

Mia hesitates for a moment then pulls her hair back away from her face and ties
it in a ponytail.

                              MIA
          The 'us' that seems to have been re-kindled here in your lovely
          city, is getting in the way of my story. The fire has gone out. You
          should have worried about us along time ago.

Kit shifts gears as he passes two trucks on the roadway.

                              KIT
          Okay... Great... Then this weekend you are out of here! I cannot
          protect you anymore.

INT: PINK BUILDING - MOMENTS LATER

Angel and Noon go back to the window. The Jeep is gone.

Angel looks down the empty roadway as from the other direction the battered
school bus approaches to pull into the yard.

INT. JEEP - ROADWAY - MINUTES LATER

                              MIA
          That was the asshole who had me attacked. Took my fucking camera!

Kit's attention stays on the road ahead.

                                  KIT
     Army mercenary. In and out of Burma, the Philippines. Drugs, women,
     guns. One day, he will either be fucking dead or rotting in some
     rat-infested jail cell.

Mia looks coldly out the car window.

                                  MIA
     I had a brief breakfast with your dickhead partner.

                              KIT (CONT'D)
     He is working with a foundation who finances some of these
     relocations. He is the our go-between.

                                  MIA

Please!

                                  KIT
     Every two, sometimes three, out of ten shipments we rescue.

A brief silence.

Mia looks like she wants to jump out of the vehicle.

                                  MIA
     On a good day, you heroically clean up a sweat-shop operation in
     the suburbs of Bangkok. On a so-so day, because of you, the police
     rescue a plane load of girls headed to some country they never
     heard of. On a not-so-good day, you and Keith receive a container
     loaded with girls dropped onto some fucking dock that who knows
     what will happen to them. And on a bad day, and how many days out
     of the week are bad days, hundreds of girls are kidnapped, sold,
     stolen....

Silence as Kit passes another semi-truck and speeds down the distant highway.

INT. PINK SCHOOL HOUSE - FOLLOWING MORNING

Angel sits across from Noon who's eating a bowl of cereal.

                                ANGEL
     How they catch you again?

Noon shacks her head no.

                                NOON
     Went to friend who told me about a good club.

Noon nods to ten-to-twelve other girls.

                              NOON (CONT'D)
          Just have to look sexy and serve drinks. No suck or fuck unless I
          want to. Guess what own by Mr. Sunglasses. Guess who runs it? That
          Joy bitch. Says now I going to be in show tonight.

Noon runs her hand through Angel's long blonde hair.

                              NOON (CONT'D)
          He make you blonde. Like American movie star.

                                ANGEL
          Sunglasses gives me pills. Drugs. (shows needle marks on her legs)
          Movies, stupid stories. I do what he asks. I don't care anymore.

Joy enters the room followed by two young boys carrying clothes. She points to
some of the girls. The boys drop the clothes at the girls feet.

Noon looks puzzled.

                              ANGEL (CONT'D)
          Those new girls. They from Vietnam. They doing show tonight.

The door opens again. Red Head along with Jimme enters the room.

She begins pointing at some of the girls. She finally comes to Noon, smiles and
motions for her to get up.

Noon gives Angel an I-told-you-so smile. Noon reaches down and tries to pull
Angel up. Jimme looks at Redhead and shakes his head no.

Noon and the rest of the chosen girls leave the room.

                                JIMME
          I think it's time for our afternoon get-together.

Jimme motions toward two other girls as Angel slowly rises and the three girls
follow Jimme down the hallway.

INT. ROOM - MINUTES LATER

Room that looks like a gym. Equipment, Yoga mats and a few massage tables. The
girls undress. FOUR CAUCASIAN MEN enter the room.

Within minutes, all parties are involved in varies sexual acts. TWO MEN with
hand=held movie cameras follow the action.

Jimme sits in the corner giving directions.

Angel is on the floor being molested by two of these men. Jimme smiles at her
and winks.

INT. PANDORA HOTEL - THAT NIGHT

Mia walks through a somewhat empty hotel lobby, scopes the surroundings, and
heads toward the elevators.

Mia sees the elevator has stopped on the 21st floor. Mia approaches the young
elevator operator.

                                  MIA
          A party tonight. Girls?

The operator shrugs his shoulders.

                                  MIA (CONT'D)
          Twenty one.

INT. HALLWAY - MOMENTS LATER

Mia enters the 21st floor hallway.

Two Asian men in black stand guard at the entrance to the ballroom.

Mia looks through a glass double door.

She enters the service area and kitchen. Mia nods to a number of workers as she
authoritatively passes through.

With her finger she tastes some of the food as she passes. She picks up a
pickle, bites a piece, makes a funny face then drops it back on the plate.

INT. BALLROOM

Mia walks casually into a grand ballroom. The room is filled with thirty to
forty guests, mostly men and a handful of women.

To her left are a number of rooms filled with tables and name cards of various
companies. There are rows of girls sitting or standing in each room.

Young males serve drinks. ELECTRO-POP drowns the conversations into an
unrecognizable BUZZ.

Mia takes a drink from a tray and walks toward a group of men standing in front
of a Victorian wall-papered wall.

They stand pondering dozens of eight-by-ten photographs of young women and
adolescent girls.

Some of the girls in the photos are completely naked or naked from the waist
up. Others look like audition photos.

Mia takes another drink from a passing waiter and tray. Jade passes her and
smiles. Jade continues toward the far side of the large stage.

Mia looks at black marker numbers scribed at the bottom of each photo.

Jimme, with drink in hand, stands a few feet behind Mia.

                                    JIMME
          Surprised to still see you here.

Jimme gives her a threatening smile.

                                    JIMME (CONT'D)
          Our conversation about you ending this heartfelt, exotic, adventure
          of yours--

                                    MIA
          Blow me.

A man in his early 50s, overweight, and with a ruddy complexion, NORM PRESCOTT,
approaches Mia.

                                    NORM
          Excuse me, I came here looking for... Oh, sorry. I'm Norm Prescott.

Mia reluctantly shakes hands with him. Norm encircles Mia.

                                    NORM (CONT'D)
          I'm the manager of a garment factory in Sri Lanka. We lost half
          of our workers after that damn wave. I overheard someone talking
          downstairs about being able to find girls who could sew.

Jimme steps between them.

                                    JIMME
          I'm sorry. You're in the wrong room. Go out the door and you will
          see a number of other rooms. Many other girls eager to work.

The music stops. A GONG is struck

Mia and Jimme turn toward the stage.

Thirty girls, some of the girls seen earlier at the school and from the
container, dressed in simple clean dresses are escorted to the stage. Each has
a printed tag number around her neck.

Joy, in a black silk, sexy night gown catwalks to center stage.

                                    JOY
          Gentlemen, Ladies. Good evening. We have here a number of lovely
          girls for you tonight. An exotic mix of Thai, Chinese, Vietnamese,
          and a few mixed breeds.

Some LAUGHTER from the crowd.

Kit approaches and stands alongside Mia.

                              JOY (CONT'D)
          These purchases are final. No returns, no damaged goods, no change
          of heart, you don't like the color, or it doesn't fit.

Some laughter from the crowd.

                                KIT
          You need to leave here right now.

Mia turns away and walks toward the other end of the large room.

Pushing one of the adjoining doors open, Mia sees a stage, with a number of
girls seated. Joy with a mic parades across the front of the stage.

In front of the stage sit rows and rows of spectators. One of the girls is now
standing a few feet away from Joy.

Joy motions towards her. She takes off her dress and is now standing in her
underwear.

                              WOMAN (O.C.)
          Number 128.

Voice from the audience.

                              VOICE (O.C.)
          250!

                          ANOTHER VOICE (O.C.)
          300!

Mia heads back into the larger ballroom. Mia stands next to Kit.

                                MIA
          Is this going to be a good day or a bad day?

CROWD

A few feet away Jade stands with Jimme.

                               JIMME
          Our Japanese friends are going to love this one. She has modern
          day Tokyo written all over her.

Mia nudges Kit.

                                MIA
          Those are the girls from the container. You fucking lied to me!

                              KIT
          They will never leave this country.

Kit turns away and walks toward Jade. Kit puts his hand on Jades shoulder.

                          KIT (CONT'D)
          They have seen the product. I'm not parading 80 girls. Yes or no?

Jade pauses then glances and smiles at the Japanese men standing left of center
in front of the stage.

Jade walks towards Japanese man and a very lovely Japanese woman who now stands
next to him.

                             JADE
          We will be putting the girls on a bus. They will be taken directly
          to the airport. Flight to leave in eight hours.

The Japanese woman, smiles and points to a dark briefcase resting on the floor
next to a large, threatening-looking Asian man standing some twenty yards away.

Jade walks toward the man. He looks at the Japanese woman who nods her head yes.

Jade turns and the Japanese woman and her companion are gone.

Jade kneels down and opens the leather bag, filled with bands of Euros.

Jade heads to the rear of the stage with the leather bag. She pauses for a
moment and stares at the two men that Keith hired to kill Mia. She takes out
her cell.

Kit takes a BEEPING cell phone from his pocket.

                          JADE (CONT'D)
          We are good... but there are two other men. Not part of the sale.
          Not Japanese. They have Ubeckie stamped all over them. Looks like
          they think it is payback time.

                              KIT
          Get the girls on the fucking bus!

STAGE

Joy and the girls quickly head off the side of the stage. FLOOR

Mia watches Joy and the girls leave the stage. Kit puts his cell away and walks
calmly toward Jimme.

                              KIT
          I've got the money and you still have the girls. Soon our Tokyo
          traders will find out what a Thai prison is like... The authorities
          are on their way.

Jimme nods and smiles.

Jimme looks at the stage. Eye contact with Joy, Jimme smiles and shacks his head yes. He turns takes a drink off a tray and exits.

The party continues.

A few yards away Kit grabs Mia by the shoulder and turns her around placing a key in her hand.

                              KIT
          Do not go back to your hotel. Go to my place. I will be back soon.
          Stay the fuck there!

Kit turns and heads toward the exit.

Mia pauses then heads toward the rear of the stage.

INT. BASEMENT - MOMENTS LATER

Mia wanders through the vast basement of pipes and equipment.

Joy and the girls are nowhere in sight.

A gun is shoved into Mia's side of her head. The two men escort Mia down a darkened concrete hallway.

                              MIA
          Get your fucking hands off of me!

An elevator opens and an older woman exits pushing a cleaning cart.

Mia pushes the woman and cart into the two men, 30 yards ahead of her is an exit. Mia breaks into a run.

The two hoods collect themselves and give chase.

EXT. BACK OF HOTEL - SAME

Joy leads the girls out the rear door of the hotel. The school bus sits some twenty yards away. Mookie opens the bus door as the girls begin to board.

EXT. SIDE STREET - SAME

Keith sits in a Range Rover watching. He looks surprised but then smiles.

                              KEITH
          That son of a bitch bought the whole flock!

EXT. REAR OF HOTEL - SAME

Mia walks in the shadows of over-hanging trees.

Mia is suddenly grabbed and a pistol placed against the back of her head.

Two quick SHOTS are fired.

INT. KEITH'S CAR - SAME TIME

Keith hears the GUN SHOTS.

                      KEITH
   Yes!

EXT. REAR OF HOTEL - SAME

Mia looks down at the two dead bodies.

The buses headlights go on and Mia stands for a moment like a deer in the headlights.

Kit steps out of the shadows with gun in hand.

INT. KEITH'S CAR - SAME

                      KEITH
   You son of a bitch!

EXT. REAR OF HOTEL - MOMENTS LATER.

Mia and Kit walk toward the bus. The bus is now loaded with all of the girls.

Mia looks in the windows at the scared but smiling faces of two of the girls.

                     KIT
   Those two. They were here to get rid of you not me. Same game plan
   but different players.

Mia looks back at the bus that is beginning to pull away.

                     MIA
   Where are the police?

                     KIT
   There is no police. All bullshit. I now have the girls and the money.

Kit motions for Mia to walk back into the shadowed area of the building. She reluctantly follows.

The bus slowly turns out onto the highway. Kit turns as a black Jeep pulls up.

Jimme smiles at Kit from the car window.

                    JIMME
   No police, Mr. Lee? I thought you were putting those Japanese in

a horrible Thai prison? What are we going to do now that we still
have the girls and their money? More important question is what
are they going to do?

Jimme's shakes his head, winks, and turns the vehicle to follows the bus.

Mia drops the key Kit gave to her earlier, turns, and walks away. She then
breaks into a run.

                              KIT

     Mia! Fuck!

INT. APARTMENT - FOLLOWING MORNING

Kit sits alone on his bed. No one else in the room. He dials his cell phone.

SPLIT SCREEN

                              KIT

     Tess.

                              TESS

     Good morning.

TESS, mid-40s and average looking, sits in a corner office. Her window overlooks
Bryant Park. On a wall to her left in large mounted silver letters, The Soros
Foundation.

                         TESS (CONT'D)
     Thought we had lost you... Okay. How can we help you?

                              KIT
     I wanted to make sure that Keith has set up the offshore account
     and--

                              TESS

     Keith?

                              KIT

     Keith Ford.

                              TESS
     Keith was killed in a nasty head-on about eight months ago in
     Beijing. From the photos we saw, it looked like a fucking Korean
     barbie. I thought you knew.

                              KIT
     But he has been... Shit! I had no idea.

                              TESS
          We hadn't heard from you in so long we thought you had jumped
          ship, or one of your trafficking buddies turned you into road kill.
          We haven't done shit since the two of you put those cock-suckers in
          Belgrade behind bars. Skin trade operations went from wholesale to
          retail to layaway... Kit? Kit?

                              KIT
          Thanks. Talk with you later. (click)

EXT. STREET OUTSIDE RESTAURANT - FOLLOWING MORNING

Mia walks through a steady rain. She removes her ringing cell phone. She Looks
at the number but does not answer. Then, she receives a text.

          TEXT - Where the hell are you? We need to talk! Call me. Kit.

Mia clicks the phone and makes a call.

                              MIA
          Alan... Shut the fuck up... Listen, someone tried to kill me... Last
          night. They're both dead... No, No. I didn't kill them!

Mia watches a police vehicle move slowly down the street. Mia looks across the
street at a Starbucks.

                              MIA
          Okay... Half hour. Starbucks.

INT. STARBUCKS - LATER

Mia sits alone in the corner.

EXT. STREET - MOMENTS LATER

A car pulls to a stop. Door opens. Mia exits Starbucks. She gets in the car.

EXT. DEAD END STREET - GUEST HOUSE - MINUTES LATER INT. CAR - CONTINUOUS

Alan pulls the car to a stop.

                              ALAN
          It's time to get the hell out of here!

                              MIA
          I went with him up into the hills north of the city. A shelter. The
          staff and children treated him like he was a saint.

The car sits idling as Mia looks out the window focusing on a cluster of young
women dressed for the night crossing the heavily trafficked street.

                              MIA (CONT'D)
     You go back.

Alan looks at Mia.

                              ALAN
     There is nothing either of us can do. She is gone. She has
     vanished, taken. Risking our lives any further is not going to
     bring her back. The number of girls on the street has nearly
     doubled.

Mia slaps him hard across the face.

                              MIA
     She's not dead!

MOMENTS LATER

Mia and Alan walk down a narrow alleyway, through a construction site.

                              ALAN
     There is a small guest house at the end of the block.

Alan pulls her into his arms and they awkwardly embrace. Mia steps back and
adjusts herself.

                              ALAN (CONT'D)
     Stay at the guest house until I call you. I'll go back to the hotel
     get your things and we will fly out of here tomorrow.

Alan kisses her softly on the lips. Mia reluctantly nods her head yes.

Alan goes back to the vehicle and removes a pistol from the glove compartment.
He walks back toward Mia.

                              ALAN (CONT'D)
     Let me show you how to use this.

Mia takes the gun, slides the clip out, back in, clicks off the safety, turns
and shoots the head of a stone monkey rested on a large stone stature of a
Buddha.

                              MIA
     I used to go to the shooting range and shoot at photos of you.
     When I was tired of killing you, I put up photos of your trophy
     girlfriend. You don't want to know the number of times I killed the
     both of you.

Alan begins to walk away.

                              MIA (CONT'D)
          There is one more thing.

Alan turns and takes a few steps back.

                              MIA (CONT'D)
          Kit is not my brother.

Alan takes a few steps towards her. She points the gun at his chest.

                              ALAN
          I knew he wasn't your brother before we left Saigon. He stayed in
          Bangkok because he knew your life would be better with me, in a
          new place with a new home. In a world far from the nightmares we
          all shared.

Alan steps back, turns and exits. Mia walks toward the guest house.

INT. GUEST HOUSE ROOM - AN HOUR LATER

The lights flicker and then go out. Thunder quietly RUMBLES.

The wind BLOWS the balcony door open. Mia slowly pulls herself out of bed.

The room is now lit only by the halo of light from the streets below.

MIRROR

Clutching the gun in both hands she points at her dark reflection in the
mirror.

Mia fires two SHOTS as the mirror shatters into pieces at her feet.

Mia picks up the phone and dials.

                              MIA
          It's me. We need to talk.

Mia picks up her hand bag and walks into the bathroom. She drops the bag onto
the floor in front of her, drops her pants, and sits down to pee.

She fumbles through the bag pulling out the memory stick she used earlier.

EXT. OBEROI HOTEL - LATER

Mia exits a taxi and heads toward the entrance to the hotel. Two police
vehicles with flashing lights block part of the driveway.

INT. NINTH FLOOR - CONTINUOUS

Mia gets off an elevator and heads toward Alan's room. A police officer stops
her in the hallway.

                              MIA
          What happened?

Two cops exit the room with a body bag on a stretcher. The bag is still open.
It's Alan.

                         POLICE OFFICER
          Male victim. A friend of yours?

                              MIA
          He is my ex... my husband.

Mia gently touches the side of Alan's face before they zip up the body bag.

Mia walks into the room. Two cops carefully do forensics on the room.

Mia picks up Alan's car keys.

                         MIA (CONT'D)
          Did you find a laptop?

The three officers shake their heads no.

                         OFFICER (O.C.)
          We are going to need to talk with you.

                              MIA
          Motherfuckers!

Mia turns and runs, almost knocking the officers with stretcher over, and down
the staircase, and out of the hotel.

INT. PARKING LOT - MOMENTS LATER

Mia sits in Alan's Jeep crying.

Monsoon rain drowns the city. Mia tries to pull herself together. She sees a
folded map on the other seat. She opens it. A red marker follows a river to a
circled location. A loose piece of paper falls out.

Mia picks up a hotel napkin and reads what is written on it.

                         MIA (V.O.)
          Alan tell your ex I know where your daughter is. Follow the
          fucking map Keith.

EXT. TRAFFIC - MINUTES LATER

Mia's Jeep moves through the heart of the city as hundreds of umbrellas form a
roof over the sidewalks.

EXT. RIVER - BOAT - LATER THAT NIGHT

The rain has turned to a glistening mist.

Mia under the protection of a canvas canopy as a small river boat slowly heads up river.

Numerous buildings: huts, hotels, floating houses, and hundreds of boats caress and illuminate the river bank.

Mia walks to the front of the boat and looks to her right.

A half mile up river a dimly-lit, old Edwardian hotel rests on top of a cliff.

Mia points as the boatman nods and turns toward the shore.

INT. POLICE HEAD QUARTERS - SAME

Kit walks into Sunee's office and closes the door.

                    KIT
     You called.

                    SUNEE
     There has been a murder at the Oberoi. The woman you're fucking's
     husband.

                    KIT
     Has she been told?

Sunee nods yes.

                    SUNEE
     She came to the hotel. They were going back to the States.

                    KIT
     Never.

Sunee drops two plane tickets on her desk.

                    SUNEE
     She left the scene before they could question her.

Kit turns and exits.

Kit stops.

                    SUNEE (CONT'D)
     Wait. Mia called here about an hour ago. She said something about
     her daughter being at the Star Dust Hotel.

                              KIT
          That is where I told Jade to take the girls... and fucking Jimme?

Kit turns and exits.

EXT. STAR DUST MOTEL - AN HOUR EARLIER

A taxi pulls up in front of the hotel. Mia exits and heads toward the entrance.

EXT. FRONT DOOR

Jimme steps out from the shadows of a large doorway.

                              MIA
          The girls?

                              JIMME
          The girls. Where's the husband?

                              MIA
          I'm going to make sure the police ask you that same question.

Mia walks past Jimme into the building, past the empty lobby, and down a narrow
hallway.

                              JIMME
          I gave you both a warning. He listened too late. Only reason you
          are still walking is I do business with your brother... And just
          waiting on the money.

Jimme motions for Mia to follow him. INT. DINING AREA - CONTINUOUS

Jimme stands as a buffer between the girls and Mia.

Mattresses, clothes, and some food litter the floor. The windows are covered
with rod-iron gates.

                              JIMME (CONT'D)
          Girls, I'd like you to meet a friend of mine.

The girls stare at Mia.

Noon, trance-like, takes a few steps toward Mia. Jimme gives Noon a threatening
smile.

                              MIA
          Noon... How are you?

                              NOON
          Good, good. We are all very lucky.

Mia looks at the other girls. Many of them girls from the hotel auction and the container.

                              MIA
          My brother told me these girls were rescued?

                              JIMME
          They were. They are not on some plane to Tokyo where God knows
          what will happen to them. Kit got the money. I got the girls
          back... And major Japanese trafficker got the message.

A YOUNG MAN, Indian, with a doctor's bag and a stethoscope dangling, exits a
bathroom followed by a GIRL who adjusts the waist string of her jalwari pants.

Mia walks toward the doctor.

                              DOCTOR
          I've got to rush. You can tell Mr. Kit that I will get the lab
          report to him first thing tomorrow morning.

Mia looks back at Jimme, turns and follows him out the door.

                              JIMME
          If I were you I would get in his car and leave with him. I'm
          playing the good guy, doing your brother a favor. There are others.
          Very, very bad guys. They won't just shoot you and leave. Shit you
          can't even imagine...

EXT. PARKING LOT

The doctor heads toward the old woman who is cooking, grabs a fresh chapati and
offers one to Mia, who refuses.

                              MIA
          The girls?

                              DOCTOR
          All are HIV clean, and all but two are virgins. The only hands that
          have touched their delicate pink flowers are mine.

He turns and heads toward his Vespa.

Mia begins to follow then turns and walks toward another vehicle.

She opens the Mercedes door, hoping to find a key. No key. She opens the car
door.

A weathered pick-up truck sits to her right.

Mia removes her cell phone and dials a number. The phone RINGS and RINGS.
Finally she speaks into the phone.

                                    MIA
              Hello? Hello. It's Mia Douglas. I'm at the Star Dust Hotel.

Gravel CRUNCHES behind Mia.

Mia cautiously moves her other hand to the back of her jacket, removing Alan's
revolver.

She quickly turns with the gun pointed Jimme's midsection.

                                MIA (CONT'D)
              All of the girls!

                                  JIMME
              He can play his guardian angel routine. I'll take the money. He
              gets our precious bouquet. Tell him to bring the fucking money!

The girls now stand a few yards behind Jimme. Another man with a gun stands at
the side of the girls.

Mia looks at the girls, going through each face second by second. Her
expression does not change.

                               JIMME (CONT'D)
              Nothing to worry about (motioning to his accomplices). She's not
              going to shoot anyone.

                                    MIA
              You're buying and selling human beings!

                                  JIMME
              We take them in off the street, feed them, find them a place to
              live. Only doing God's work.

The other gunman raise his gun and places it to the side of Noon's head.

Mia turns and drops the other man with a shot to the head.

                                    MIA
              The keys to the fucking truck!

Another hood moves quietly behind Mia. But not quiet enough. Mia turns and with
one SHOT drops the hood behind her.

                                  JIMME
              You stupid bitch!

                                    MIA
              The good Lord just made me their fucking guardian angel!

Mia points the gun at Jimme's head.

                              JIMME
          Okay. Okay.

He tosses her the keys.

                              MIA
          Lie down on the ground and put your arms out to the side. Like
          you're crucified, like you should be!

Jimme falls to the ground.

                              MIA (CONT'D)
          You move, and I put a bullet in your fucking head.

Mia looks at Noon.

                              MIA (CALMLY) (CONT'D)
          Tell the girls to get into the truck!

The girls stand looking at her as if she is an apparition. Noon looks at the
girls but stands frozen.

                              MIA (CONT'D)
          Tell them to get in the back of the damn truck! Now!

Noon turns slowly and repeats what Mia has just said.

A few of the girls head for the truck. One GIRL deviates from the group and
approaches Jimme.

                              GIRL
          I can't go home. They will kill me!

Mia looks at her and then back at Jimme.

                              MIA
          What I want to do is put a bullet in your--

                              JIMME
                         (softly to Mia)
          You're risking your life for these fucking girls that nobody gives
          a flying fuck about. When are you going to understand you're
          fucking with some--

                              MIA
          Very very bad people. I guess that's the line that is supposed to
          make me piss in my panties. Tell these very, very bad people that

                    I have their fucking laundry list, and I'm taking it to some very,
                    very dedicated cleaners.

Mia turns quickly and FIRES A SHOT putting a bullet in the center of a statue
of a seated Buddha some twenty yards away.

Mia back steps toward the truck as Noon opens the rear cargo door.

TRUCK

Mia shifts into reverse, into drive, and speeds onto the roadway.

Jimme rises and takes out his cell phone. Angrily, he turns and heads to the
house screaming into the phone.

                              JIMME
                    Keith, you motherfucker! She took the fucking girls!

EXT. RURAL ROAD - MERCEDES - MOMENTS LATER

A young man drives with Jimme, in the passenger seat holding a gun.

EXT. MIA'S TRUCK - MOMENTS LATER

The girls are being tossed around in he rear of the truck. Some try to hold on.

Mia looks out the mirror nothing. She continues to drive. Looks again
headlights illuminate he road behind her.

A vehicle now seen in her rear view mirror.

INT. TRUCK - SAME

Jimme empties a clip at the fleeing truck.

INT. MIA'S TRUCK - CONTINUOUS

Noon slides down into the seat as bullets shatter the rear window.

                              MIA
                    (screams at the girls) Stay down!

EXT. CAR CHASE - SAME

Jimme tries to pass them, but Mia cuts him off. More SHOTS are fired. Mia turns
and fires out the side window.

The chase continues.

INT. SUN' CAR

The truck lunges to the left, SLAMMING into the side of the Mercedes. Jimme
fights to maintain control.

Additional SHOTS fired.

Seconds later, the truck hits an open ditch, spins, and jerks to a dead stop.

Mia descends from the truck with gun in hand.

Noon walks slowly behind Mia. The other girls huddle in the rear of the truck. One of the girls is bleeding. A few are sobbing.

Jimme walks toward her with a rifle in hand. He fires two shots into the ground on either side of her.

                              JIMME
          Don't worry. Shooting you would be to easy.

Mia points the gun at Jimme and fires. CLICK, CLICK.

                         JIMME (CONT'D)
          If you're going to play with firearms you should know how many
          rounds they carry. Even if you had a full clip...

Mia stands frozen.

Mia pulls the trigger again. CLICK.

Jimme hits her firmly in the face, knocking her to the ground.

Jimme rounds up the girls.

                         JIMME (CONT'D)
          Let's go back to my place and make some lemonade.

EXT. ROADWAY - MINUTES LATER

The girls walk back down the highway illuminated by the head lights of the vehicle behind them.

INT. CAR - SAME

Jimme and Mia set in the back set of the Mercedes.

                              JIMME
          How poetic. A truck load of lovely young lambs going back to their
          barn.

Jimme looks at Mia and smiles.

                         JIMME (CONT'D)
          And you want to take the fun out of it.

Mia spits in his face. Jimme punches Mia in the face.

Mia bleeds from the nose and mouth as her head rests against the car window.

INT. HOTEL - EMPTY HOTEL DINING AREA - LATER

Mia tries unsuccessfully to pull herself free as two men duct tape her to a chair in the center of the room.

                              MIA
          I need something to drink.

Jimme picks up a water bottle, opens it, and pours the entire bottle into her mouth and nose. She repeatedly gags.

                              JIMME
          Up until now you have been a very lucky lady.

He slaps her hard across the face.

                              JIMME (CONT'D)
          Later tonight we are going to have ourselves a party. You and the
          boys. Twenty, maybe twenty-five, of my best chums. We'll have a
          little wine, due some coke, and then you are going to have a very
          private intimate moment with each one of them.

MOMENTS LATER

Jimme pushes a metal cart toward Mia.

                              JIMME
          Mookie!

Mookie walks into the room.

                              JIMME (CONT'D)
          You do remember Mr. Roadkill? I think it's time to loosen her up a
          little bit. Get the juices flowing.

Mookie leans forward and licks her face. Mia tries to bit him. He rips open her shirt.

Mookie smiles and pulls the cart closer. The cart carries a small battery with jumper cables.

Jimme sits in a large leather chair about fifteen feet in front of Mia.

                              JIMME (CONT'D)
          We are going to start with a low voltage.

Mookie begins to pull off Mia's pants.

                              JIMME (CONT'D)
      Did I say anything about undressing her. We are trying to keep
      this respectable.

Keith comes out of nowhere and pulls Mookie away, hitting him across the head
with his pistol.

Keith looks at Jimme, surmising that things may soon get out of control.

Keith and Mia stare at each other.

                                KEITH
      She's supposed to be dead!

Mookie gets up and walks toward Jimme.

                                MOOKIE
      Look at the rage in her eyes.

Keith turns back to Mia

                              KEITH (SOFTLY)
      I'm going to get you out of this.

Keith turns and SHOOTS Mookie in the head.

                              KEITH (CONT'D)
      I've been wanting to do that for a such a long time.

Keith turns around and points the gun at Jimme.

                              KEITH (CONT'D)
      You did exactly what I told you not to do. She called the police
      over an hour ago. If I were you, I would take the girls and get
      the fuck out of here.

INT. BLACK LIMO - MINUTES LATER

The black limo moves quickly along the rural highway.

                                KEITH
      So, it looks like I saved your ass again. Your laptop.

Keith looks straight out the windshield.

                              KEITH (CONT'D)
      From what we found on your laptop, it looked like you were ready
      to, as we say, clear the playing field.

                              MIA
          I thought that was the game plan. And Kit knew nothing about it.

Keith looks at his reflection in the rear view mirror.

                             KEITH
          Kit was beginning to see that the more times you cross that
          dividing line in the middle of the highway the more it begins to
          disappear to a point where it eventually vanishes.

Keith removes the BEEPING cell phone from his pocket.

                         KEITH (CONT'D)
          Son of a bitch... Goddamn. Find the son of a bitch.

                         MIA (SOFTLY)
          You're going to kill Kit?

The driver begins to slow down as Keith turns and smiles at Mia.

                             KEITH
          As you should already know, I've never been much of a team player.

Keith lights a cigarette.

                         KEITH (CONT'D)
          The most important men in your life will be dead... Your G.I. Joe
          ex-husband followed you here and now has two bullet holes in his
          head. Your brother, once a good friend of mine, was willing to risk
          everything including his life for you... Soon he will be dead.

The driver looks at Mia, then at Keith.

                         KEITH (CONT'D)
          Death certificates with their names written in your blood.

Keith puts on his sunglasses and glares out the front window. He motions for
the driver to slow down.

                         KEITH (CONT'D)
          Kind of Shakespearean. Two male lovers dead because of the woman
          they both loved with the love that was fatally reciprocated.

                              MIA
          Where is my daughter?

                             KEITH
          We all hope that she is in heaven with the fucking angels but
          payback can be a real bitch. I can't imagine how hard it must be to

everyday think about where she may be. Is she dead or alive? What
someone may be doing to her...

Mia tries to attack Keith from the back seat. He pulls a revolver and puts it
against her forehead.

                         KEITH (CONT'D)
         One day, I think it was in Kabul... You told me how much your
         lovely daughter wanted a puppy. When you got back from Thailand
         you and her daddy were going to get her one... We went to a lot of
         trouble to get her one a few weeks earlier. And I don't even like
         dogs. But with a Chinese cook that knows what they are doing, they
         can make a really tasty stew.

Keith and Mia glare at each other.

                         MIA
         You motherfucker! I will...

The driver turns up the radio as the vehicle suddenly stops.

                         DRIVER
         Not in the fucking car.

Keith opens the car door with his gun pointed at Mia's head.

                         KEITH
         Let's go, sweetheart! It is time for our Lady Macbeth to pay for
         her crimes and misdemeanors.

The driver rolls down his window and lights a cigarette.

Keith turns, toward a view of a field being plowed by a young boy, two oxen and
his father.

                         KEITH (CONT'D)
         How picturesque. Something to send back home to Mom and Dad. Get
         out of the fucking car!

Keith stands between the back seat and the open car door. He motions with his
revolver for her to exit.

Mia hesitates as her left hand goes to the back of her pants.

                         KEITH (CONT'D)
         Not like the photos you set home. Death, destruction, injustice,
         murder and those awful out-of-focus photos of me and the 14-year-
         old getting it doggie-style against the tailgate of a U.N. Jeep.
         Good try my dear. What worries me now is that with today's
         technology you could play with those images and make out who the
         horrible fat fuck was...

Mia slowly begins to exit.

A huge semi-truck noisily rushes past their vehicle. GUN SHOTS.

The black limo idles at the side of the road.

Keith lies on the ground with a bullet in his chest. The driver lies against
the steering wheel with a bullet hole to the back of his head.

Mia turns and FIRES two more rounds into each of them.

Mia puts on the flashing lights on the limo and puts up the driver side tinted
window. Mia puts the gun in the back of her pants.

EXT. TWO LANE BLACKTOP - MINUTES LATER.

A battered pick-up stops next to the limo. Mia motions that something is wrong
with the vehicle, acts exasperated and gets into the truck.

The truck continues toward down the two lane highway.

EXT. BANGKOK STREET - MORNING

Mia maneuvers through pedestrian traffic and stops in front of a computer cafe.

INT. COMPUTER CAFE - CONTINUOUS

Mia talks with a youth in a baseball cap. He points to an empty table and monitor.

The guy then points to the far corner of the establishment.

INT. BATHROOM - MOMENTS LATER

Typical shoddy pedestrian bathroom.

Mia goes into the stall. With her pants at her knees she squats to pee, puts
her hand between her legs, grimaces, and then pulls out the memory stick.

Mia picks up a piece of toilet paper from the floor and wipes off the device.

Mia picks the revolver up off the floor and drops the gun into the hanging
water tank.

INT. TABLE WITH MONITOR - MOMENTS LATER

Mia inserts the memory stick.

INT. BLACK LIMO - SAME

Slender female hand with blue nails holds a cell phone.

IMAGE ON CELL PHONE.

Quick pan of side of Japanese airliner. Cut to shot of bus doors being opened.
Jade steps out as the girls from the auction leave the bus. The camera follows

the girls as they climb the ramp and enter the open entrance of the jet.

Jade turns around and nods to two pilots, one looks like a woman as they enter behind the girls. She tuns and does a thumbs up to the camera.

INT. LIMO - SAME

Face of the Japanese woman seen earlier at the auction. She smiles and motions for the driver to leave their hotel parking lot.

Close up again of her cell phone. The delicate hand types in bank info and with in seconds $250,000 is transferred to Kit's Overseas Placement account.

EXT. AIRPORT. HOUR LATER.

Private jet sits alone in front of open hanger. Lights on the interior of the plane are off.

Black limo pulls up to the side of a private jet.

Two men pushing ramp up to side of the jet and set the ramp.

Limo doors open. Woman and the three men seen earlier exit the limo and begin their assent to the aircraft. The two heavies follow the woman and man up the stairs.

Their limo pulls away.

The Japanese woman enters the aircraft. Lights are flicked on.

The Japanese woman and her companion stop in stride.

The entire inside of the aircraft is filled with the girls from the bus.

EXT. Tarmac - CONTINUOUS

Suddenly lights from four different vehicles flood the tarmac and light up the private jet like a Christmas tree.

Police vehicles, SIRENS BLARING quickly encircle the private jet.

Sunee and four other police with guns drawn head for the ramp. Kit steps out of another vehicle and follows.

The two Japanese heavies on the ramp turn and open firs. Shots are fired as the two heavies tumble to the pavement.

Sunee, gun drawn, enters the aircraft. The Japanese woman and her accomplice sit motionless in the two front empty seats of the airplane.

Two police come in behind Sunee.

One of them has a body camera and films the interior of the aircraft.

                              SUNEE
          Arrest them for the trafficking of human beings.

Sunee walks to the still seated woman and puts the barrel of her pistol against
the woman's perfect red lips.

The cockpit door opens and Jade walks out behind Sunee. Jade nods her head yes.

                              JADE
          The money has been wired.

                              SUNEE
I can only imagine what they will do to this bitch when she is behind bars.

Jade looks out the open door way and down the ramp. An officer is bending over
Kit who lies on the tarmac bleeding.

                              JADE
          Fuck!

Jade heads down the ramp.

INT. HOTEL LOBBY - SAME NIGHT

Mia walks into the lobby of her hotel. She is about to get on the elevator when
she sees Prescott and another man get up from a table, exit the restaurant and
head out of the hotel.

Mia walks to their table, flips the hotel receipt and sees the room number.

Mia looks at the elevator.

INT. HALLWAY

Mia walks down a long corridor.

A young cleaning woman exits a room behind her.

Mia unsuccessfully Prescott's room door. Mia turns back toward the woman.

                              MIA
          I'm sorry. I left my key in my room.

The young woman hesitates. Mia seems helpless. The young woman smiles and opens
the door for Mia.

                              MIA (CONT'D)
          Thank you.

INT. HOTEL ROOM - MOMENTS LATER

Mia slowly walks though Prescott's hotel room.

Open suitcase's clothes in closet and over chairs. A couple of liquor bottles.
Some sex toys at the foot of the bed.

Handcuffs on a side table.

Half-filled container of lubricant on bathroom sink along with a pack of
Trojans.

She picks up a camera off the floor by the side of the bed.

Mia is about to sit down on the bed but hesitates and walks toward the small
terrace with the camera in hand. Taking a deep breath, she looks down at the
busy spider web of streets below.

Mia begins to flip through the camera photos. Her expression turns from disgust
to horror. There is a quick glimmer of a video. Tears fill her eyes.

INT. HALLWAY DOOR - POLICE STATION - FOLLOWING DAY

A female's hands KNOCK on a door.

Sunee stands on the other side of the open door. Sunee smiles.

MOMENTS LATER

Mia and Sunne sit across from each other at a table, alone in what looks like a
interrogation room.

Photos are mounted on the wall behind Sunee.

                              SUNEE
          The girls are safe.

Sunee looks at Mia then at two officers within hearing distance. Sunee smiles
and leans over the desk.

                         SUNEE (CONT'D)
          Kit was...

                              MIA
          Is he...

                              SUNEE
          No, but in serious condition. Luckily, he had his vest on. Two of
          the shots would have killed him.

                              MIA
          My daughter?

                              SUNEE

     We spent months after you left looking for her. So did your
     brother. I was rookie then... Girls missing, vanishing, is an
     everyday event in Bangkok. If missing for more than six weeks, they
     either don't want to be found, are set-up so they never will be
     found or as with your daughter, well, they are assumed dead. Most
     cold cases here end up in the what we call the freezer.

Tears streak Mia's face as she motions for Sunee to stop.

Mia removes Prescott's camera from her bag.

                               MIA

     I have something to show you.

Mia clicks on the cell phone.

                           MIA (CONT'D)

I went through these guys hotel room. Some pretty wired shit. Then I found
this.

SCREEN OF CELL PHONE - VIDEO EXT. PINK BUILDING - EVENING

Camera scans front of building.

                          PRESCOTT (V.O.)

     Stop with your worrying. Bill, this is fucking Thailand, not
     fucking Cleveland.

Prescott turns the cellphone toward his partner, BILL, another 60-year-old, with
what looks like a Johnnie Depp hair piece on his head. Bill motions that he
does not want to be filmed. Prescott hands him the camera.

Door opens. They are escorted into a medium-sized room. Against a far wall
stand eight-to-ten teenage girls.

                            MIA (V.O.)

     The one wearing the rug... I have no who he is or what he does.
     The other son-of-a-bitch was at the auction. Last name is... I
     think Prescott. Claimed he was looking for workers for his sneaker
     factory.

The camera follows as Prescott begins to undress. He laughs and covers his
genitals.

The camera turns to a teenager who is now taking off her clothes in front of a
bed.

Bill drops his pants as he awkwardly films the two girls now on their knees in
front of him.

Bill now sweeps the room with the cell phone. The other young girl is sitting spread-legged on Prescott's lap.

                              BILL
          Not sure how much more I can film of this. Shit... You were right
          about not being Cleveland.

A close up of the girls' faces. Then the video jumps quickly to another Thai male who enters the frame carrying a real movie camera.

On the other side of the frame sit two older teenage girls.

INT. POLICE OFFICE - CONTINUOUS

Mia freezes on the other two girls. Mia enlarges the image.

                              MIA
          The girl on the left.

Mia takes the folded photo from her pocket and drops it onto the table.

                              SUNEE
          The blond girl?

Sunne picks up the photograph and compares the photo to the image on the screen.

Both women look at each other then both go back to viewing the cell phone video.

CONTINUOUS VIDEO

Prescott suddenly motions for the Thai not to film him. Bill follows the confrontation with the video.

                              BILL (V.O.)
          No one said this was going to be filmed by anyone?

Suddenly from behind the Thai cameraman, Jimme comes through the door, yells and screams. The Thai cameraman follows Jimme. Jimme is dressed in a police officers uniform and carrying a gun he turns in a sweeping motion as he yells and threatens the two men.

                              JIMME
          What the fuck is going on here? Are you fucking kidding me.

The Thai cameraman follows Jimme.

Bill continues to film as he tries to pull up his pants.

Bill films, his hand shaking as Jimme puts the gun to the head of the Prescott.

Behind Jimme, another Thai with a brush, paints red marks on two of the girls heads and breast.

                              PRESCOTT
          We are doing nothing illegal. This is fucking Thailand!

Jimme knocks Prescott to the ground with a fist to the head.

Another YOUNG THAI male tosses underwear on the floor, a few empty beer bottles, wasted fruit.

The girls fall around Prescott as he now tries to get to his feet.

Jimme is obviously stoned and or drunk. He fires two shots into the floor around Prescott.

The Thai cameraman moves in to a close-up of Jimme then a quick turn back to the girls on the floor.

The girls on the floor look like they have been beaten and abused.

                              JIMME
          These girls are not even 13-years-old! Children! We do have laws!
          Look what you have done to them!

Jimme forcefully pulls Prescott to a standing position and motions for the Thai with the camera to sop filming.

The Thai camera man stops filming.

                          JIMME (CONT'D)
          Tell you what... I'm going to be a nice guy.

Bill's video now focus on Jimme and Prescott. Jimme staggers for a moment.

                          JIMME (V.O.)
                       (DeNiro type voice)
          Your fucking wallets and watches!

Prescott removes his wallet, and expensive watch, and hands them one of the younger Thai men.

The video camera lowers to a quick image of the girls on the floor, then a THUD. Image visually muddled.

The visual comes back on as someone has picked up the cell phone.

Suddenly, an out of focus selfie of Angel, then an image of Jimme taking money from Prescott's wallet. Video blurs, then a shuffling image of the Bill's pants and his back pocket.

The cell video image goes black.

POLICE OFFICE - CONTINUOUS

                              MIA
         The asshole with the sunglasses.

                              SUNEE
         Jimme Thon, your brother deals with him. Ex-militia whack-job.
         Burma, Philippines, Cambodia. Traffics in about everything. Often
         to keep the peace, he turns over shipments of trafficked girls.

                              MIA
         I think he had me attacked on the street and had my husband
         killed!

Mia clicks back through the video and stops at the image of the front of the
building.

                              SUNNE
         Cheap beach motel... Many of them all along southern coast.

                              MIA
         I know where it is.

Mia enlarges the image and edits to a blurred sign.

                              MIA (CONT'D)
         The Frangipani.

Sunee heads toward another room, motions for Mia to stay at the door. Sunne
shows the photos to several other officers, one goes to his laptop and does a
Google search.

Sunne steps out of the room.

                              SUNEE
         Yes, but not within Bangkok jurisdiction. Close to 200 miles
         from here.

(MORE)

                              SUNEE (CONT'D)
         Those girls probably have never worked in Bangkok... Main reason
         your daughter was not found. The strip along the beach is a whole
         different scene.

Sunee walks past Mia.

Mia reaches out and grabs her turning Sunee around.

                                    MIA
          That girl... The blond in the photo that is my daughter. I will go
          there myself!

Tears streak Mia's face as both women stare at each other as Mia steps around
her and leaves the office.

EXT. VILLAGE - LATER THAT NIGHT

Two vehicles pull up at the front of the motel. Headlights off. Full moon
illuminates the front of the motel. A few people still walk the dimly-lit beach.

Two additional vehicles jerk to a stop at the other side of building.

Sunee removes a silencer from her glove box and snaps it on to her gun.

Sunee exits the vehicle as three other police officers pull weapons and head
toward the front door. Two other officers go around back.

Dogs begin barking. A light goes on. Two officers SMASH in the front door.

Mia along with another officer follow Sunee into the small lobby. Joy sits
behind the reception desk. She suddenly gets up from the desk holding a gun.
Sunee takes her down with one silent shot to the head.

Two hoods stumble out of an adjoining room and are taken down with gun SHOTS
from another officer. Another comes out pointing a gun and is SHOT by Sunee.

INT. HALLWAY - REAR DOOR - CONTINUOUS

Sunee forces open a locked door. Inside the room are six-or-seven make shift
beds and fifteen-to-twenty teenage girls, girls we have seen before.

INT. ANOTHER ROOM - CONTINUOUS

Mia follows Sunee into another room and looks hopefully at each one of the girls.

                                   SUNEE
          We are the police. Good police.

A few of the girls sit motionless. Police officers enter and attempt to remove
the girls. A number of the girls try to escape by fighting back.

                              SUNEE (CONT'D)
          We are here to take you away. You will be safe.

One of the girls really fights back, hitting and biting the officer trying to
help her.

INT. ROOM DOWN THE HALL - SAME

Mia enters another room. The room is littered with lights, two movie cameras, and a makeshift interior with a bed and sofa. The room that was seen in the cell phone video.

Framed tacky erotic prints hang over the sofa and a clothes rack rests in the far corner. Under the rack of clothes rests a number of dildos and handcuffs.

Mia separates costumes hanging on the clothes cart. Suddenly she is hit from behind on the side of the head.

SECONDS LATER

Angel stands at the open door, looking at Mia on the floor. Jimme steps out from behind the door and grabs Angel.

INT. HALLWAY - CONTINUOUS

Jimme steps over one of the dead Thai hoods with a gun held to the side of Angel's head.

                         JIMME
          Get the fuck out of my way!

INT. MAIN ROOM - CONTINUOUS

With Angel in his grasp, Jimme back steps towards the front door.

                         JIMME
          Put the fucking guns down!

                         SUNEE
          Let her go!

                         JIMME
          Put the guns down or I give my little angel fucking wings!

Sunee and the other two cops reluctantly drop their weapons.

Behind Jimme, a male hand picks a revolver from the floor.

Jimme is a few steps away from the front door.

A GUN SHOT as Jimme jerks forward with a bullet hole in his back.

Jimme staggers then falls. Angel stands frozen, looking down at Jimme's body.

INT. HALLWAY - SAME

Mia staggers out from the room where she was attacked.

At the other end of the hall, Kit stands with gun in hand pointed at Jimme
still lying on the floor.

Kit and Mia exchange a glance, Kit turns and exits.

Angel slowly bends down and touches the side of Jimme's face. Mia moves towards
Angel.

                              ANGEL
          What have they done to you?

                         JIMME (THAI)
          My sweet Angel. Tell them how I have taken care of you.

Angel picks up the revolver and stands holding the gun in both hands.

                         ANGEL (SOFTLY)
          My name is Asia.

Mia turns with the gun pointed at Sunee.

Mia slowly walks towards Asia.

                              MIA
          Asia... No, no... She helped me find you.

Angel turns and points the gun at Mia. Jimme tries to get up from the floor.

                             JIMME
          Tell them, my angel. They have the wrong man. I was like a
          father to you.

Asia points the gun at Jimme's head.

                             ASIA
          I never told you my real name. My name is Asia. My name is Asia.

Jimme smiles and reaches out to his angel.

                         ASIA (CONT'D)
          I was never your Angel. I was sometimes your schoolgirl, daughter,
          girlfriend... your wife, your whore, your nurse, but always a
          prisoner and your slave! What I wanted to be most of all is what I
          am now...

Asia turns back towards Mia and Sunee.

                         ASIA (CONT'D)
          Your killer!

Mia shakes her head no as she walks towards her daughter.

Asia looks at Mia, shrugs her shoulders, and fires three times into Jimme's head.

Mia takes a few steps closer as Asia now places the gun to the side of her own head.

                              MIA
          Asia, we have found you. Please, you are my daughter...

A brief stand-off.

Mia steps forward and carefully removes the gun from Asia's hand. Asia turns and walks toward the open door.

Mia lets the gun fall to the floor.

EXT. FRONT OF BUILDING - CONTINUOUS

The other girls, still unclear of what has just happened, are escorted toward an ambulance and police van.

Asia breaks into a run for the beach.

A few traffickers are handcuffed and forcefully removed from the building. Police interrogate villagers.

EXT. BEACH - SAME

Sunne and Mia exchange a heartfelt smile and an embrace.

BEACH - CONTINUOUS

Mia approaches Asia who is now standing knee-high in surf. Mia reaches out and tries to pull Asia into her arms.

Asia hesitates and pulls away.

                              ASIA
          They told me that you left me! That you did not want me anymore!

                              MIA
          Someone stole you. They took you away from us.

                              ASIA
          I told the girls that my mother was dead. Why did you take so
          long?

                              MIA
          We looked for you for over a year. The police have continued to
          look for you. Those men took you far away. But we have found you.

EXT. ROADWAY - SAME

The yellow school bus pulls into the parking lot. Girls from the auction begin to exit.

Noon approaches Sunne. Sunne hesitates then points to the beach.

Noon walks to the roadway then stops.

EXT. BEACH - SAME

Asia watches as the girls exit the bus.

                    ASIA
          What about the other girls?

Noon waves, Asia waves back. Mia turns back toward the bus and girls.

                    ASIA (CONT'D)
          Noon, her name is Noon. She told me about a crazy woman with a
          photograph.

                    MIA
          We will make sure she is taken care of.

Asia pulls away and stares at her mother. Mia sobbing pulls her back into her arms.

                    MIA (CONT'D)
          You were in my heart, in my thoughts every minute of every day.

Mia and Asia walk along the beach under a star filled sky.

                    MIA (CONT'D)
          We thought we would never see you again.

BEACH - CONTINUOUS

                    ASIA
          I killed the man who took care of me. He took care of me bad,
          sometimes good. He told me to treat him like he was my father. To
          do what he told me. He made me do things. I was going to be his
          movie star. He gave me drugs. I had sex over and over. Look at my
          hair. He said Hollywood stars have blonde hair.

Asia stops and takes a few steps away from her mother.

                    ASIA (CONT'D)
          I'm so sorry. He made me do terrible things. Why would you want me?

For the first time Asia begins to cry.

INT. JEEP - SIDE ROAD - CONTINUOUS

Kit watches as Mia and Asia continue their walk on the beach.

EXT. BEACH - SAME

Asia falls back into Mia's arms.

                              ASIA
          Please forgive me. You have saved my life.

                              MIA
          Nothing to forgive. You have survived. We have found you. No one
          will hurt you again.

                              ASIA
          Where is my father?

                              MIA
          He is.... We will talk about that later... We may see him soon.

JEEP - SAME

Kit looks down the moon-lit beach as the surf caresses Mia and Asia, embraced
in each others arms.

BEACH - CONTINUOUS

Over Mia's shoulder Asia watches Kit's jeep in the dark shadows of the trees
pull out onto the roadway and speed away.

INT. SOROS FOUNDATION - MORNING - TWO DAYS LATER

Tess drinks her Starbucks as she clicks through her e-mails. She turns to see
who else is in the office.

                              TESS
          Brad.

BRAD, in his early 50s, with a three-day-old beard and a Ramones t-shirt walks
toward her.

                              BRAD
          What's the problem?

Tess scrolls through pages of thumbnail photos of girls and young women. A
written page fills the screen. Tess begins to read:

                              MIA (V.O)
          What you're looking at is a sampling of girls and young women
          who have been bought, sold, stolen, kidnapped, raped, beaten, and

sometimes murdered. A small sampling of the tens of thousands
of young people who are sold into the skin trade everyday. This
traffic has no borders, no ethic, racial or religious prejudice.
The countries they come from are most of the United Nations. All
you have to be is young, female and or male and made available
due to the economic, social, and cultural negatives that may have
impacted your life.

                         TESS
          Over 50 pages. Girls from 12-15 different countries, and I just got
          started.

                         BRAD
          This certainly gives a whole new meaning to Facebook.

                         TESS
          Brad you are fucking dickhead!

Tess continues to read.

                         MIA (V.O)
          On the following page you will see financial records, e-mail
          addresses, company names, political organizations, and in some
          cases specific names of many of these gangsters and criminals.
          It's time to try and find girls like these, to rescue these girls.
          It's time to stop this horror, and put these motherfuckers out of
          business, behind bars and if necessary, dead.

                         BRAD
          Who sent this?

                         TESS
          For their sake they did not leave a clue other then a web address:
          SearchingforAsia.com.

EXT. HOTEL TERRACE - A MONTH LATER

A gentle breeze sweeps over the terrace.

Mia's new laptop is open to one of the typed pages just seen. A memory stick
lies on the table next to the laptop. There is a KNOCK on the room door,
another KNOCK.

TERRACE - SAME

Mia's folder flips open.

Gracefully a number of Mia's photos of the girls gets carried off with the
breeze and into the clear sky and over the hotel swimming pool. Mia is teaching

Asia how to swim in the crystal clear water of the pool. Asia's hair is no
longer blonde.

OVERVIEW

At the other end of the pool, Noon and a number of the girls from the bus are
either pool side or in the water.

OVERVIEW - SLOW PULLOUT

Ten yards from the side of the pool Kit sits in a beach chair.

A cell-phone rings.

Behind Kit on the hotel wall above a row of tall palm trees is a sign that
reads - Old Saigon Hotel - Ho Chi Minh City - Vietnam.

Kit reaches into the bag and removes a revolver as he rises and places a gun,
also from the bag, into the back waistband of his slacks.

Kit walks slowly to the edge of the pool area that looks out over the vast city.
The phone rings again. Kit answers it.

FADE TO BLACK

From 1965 to present, artist **Garey Riester** has lived in four states and three countries in a total of 54 different locations and 14 different studios. He has completed more than 750 works of art, without the inclusion of art prints and photographs. More than 150 pieces of his art have sold, and resold at auctions, and belong to more than 60 private collections and hang in several museums.

His screenplays have been in about two dozen festivals and optioned twice. He was once represented by the Gersh Agency in New York City.